Malcolm Stuart Taylor, Anne Lindsay Barnard

Auld Robin Gray

An Emotional Drama

Malcolm Stuart Taylor, Anne Lindsay Barnard

Auld Robin Gray
An Emotional Drama

ISBN/EAN: 9783337343200

Printed in Europe, USA, Canada, Australia, Japan

Cover: Foto ©Andreas Hilbeck / pixelio.de

More available books at **www.hansebooks.com**

AN EMOTIONAL DRAMA,

IN FIVE ACTS,

— BY —

MALCOLM STUART TAYLOR,

AUTHOR OF

An Afflicted Family, "*Aar-u-ag-oos,*" *A Fool's Errand, Etc.*

———

From the famous Scotch Ballad of the same name by **Lady Anne** Barnard.

———

Printed from the original manuscript, with the stage business carefully marked, relative positions, Etc.

———

———

—— CLYDE, OHIO: ——
A. D. AMES, PUBLISHER.

AULD ROBIN GRAY.

CHARACTERS REPRESENTED.

Robin Gray	of Cairnieford
Jeamie Falcon	a young Farmer
Nicol McWhapple	of Clashgirn
Adam Lindsay	a Fisherman
Mathew Smart	the Fiscal
Andrew Monduff	the Minister
Luke Carnegie	a Lawyer
Wattie Todd	a Simpleton
Ivan Carrach	Skipper of the Colin
Hutcheson	his First Mate
Donald	a Sailor
Sandy } David }	Fishermen
Jeannie Lindsay	Jeamie's Lass
Margaret Lindsay	her invalid Mother
Girzie Todd	a Fishwife

Sailors, Peasants and Fishermen.

COSTUMES.

ROBIN.—First and second act, farmer's suit of corduroy—cutaway coat—low waistcoat—knee breeches—Scotch bonnet—ribbed woolen stockings—buckled shoes—plain shirt and kerchief. Third and following acts. Black frock coat—red vest—black breeches—white ruffled bosom shirt—black neckcloth and a staff—looks disordered in last act.

JEAMIE.—First Act. Plowboy's suit like Robin's first, but of poorer quality. Third and last Act. Sailor's suit—white jacket—blue shirt with broad collar and cuffs—blue neck-kerchief—white trousers and broad brimmed straw hat.

NICOL.—Full suit of black, like Robin's—white stockings and neckcloth—black three-cornered hat—snuff box and staff.

ADAM.—Fisherman's suit—red flannel shirt—blue flannel short loose trousers—tarpaulin hat—blue neck-cloth and a fishing net.

MATHEW }
ANDREW } Something like Nicol's, but not so sombre looking.
LUKE }

WATTIE.—A Highlander's suit—jacket and kilt, pretty well worn out.

IVAN.—Sailor's suit—jacket and trousers of blue flannel—red striped shirt with broad collar—red flannel night-cap—broad leather belt.

HUTCHESON.—The same, with blue shirts and Scotch bonnets.
DONALD. "   "   "   "   "   "

SANDY and DAVID.—The same as Adam's.

JEANNIE.—First Act.—Scotch lassie's dress—blue tight-fitting waist—short kilted skirt—Scotch cap and scarf all of plaid goods, plain knit stockings, and slippers. Third Act.—House-wife's dress of white, with low neck and short sleeves, the skirt looped up at back, showing long fancy striped petticoat. Last Act.—Dress of drab or gray, with white kerchief pinned across breast.

MRS. LINDSAY.—Invalid's loose wrapper.

GIRZIE.—Fishwife's dress—man's straw hat—linsey-woolsey waist, and kilted skirt, looped up back, showing fancy red flannel petticoat—ribbed woolen stockings—heavy shoes—small plaid shawl crossed in front and tied behind—basket of fish slung on back.

Auld Robin Gray.

ACT I.

SCENE FIRST. — The Port. Coast in the background; the ship "Colin," at dock, ready to sail. Boxes, barrels and bales on either side. Sailors discovered loading the vessel. Girzie Told, Sandy and Hutchison, talking. Donald among the sailors.

Girzie. (*crying her fish*) Herrin'! Fine fresh herrin'! Fresh from the hook! (*Solo introduced, "Caller Herrin."*)

Sailors. (*loading the vessel*) Heave, ho! Heave, ho!

Hutch. Heave ahead, my hearties!

Girzie. What are ye all astir for?

Hutch. Do you not see we are about to set sail?

Girzie. Not the day?

Hutch. Yes, this very hour.

Girzie. But man, this is Friday.

Hutch. Carrach swore, pe-tam, we would sail with to-day's tide whether it was Friday or Saturday.

Donald. (*coming down*) I'll not go with him anyway, for it's just flying in the face of Providence.

Girzie. Aye, man, Ivan Carrach was aye known to be ready to flee in the face o' Providence, or any ither body that was in his way. But there's a storm brewing yonder in the lift, that'll maybe make him be sorry for't this time.

Don. Well, I'll not go with him, that I'm resolved on.
(*exit* L. 1 E.

Girzie. An' nae ane will blame ye. But where's that boy Wattie, gone?

Hutch. I saw him wandering up the road leading the donkey cropping the grass.

Girzie. De'il tak' the creature! He's a hantle mair trouble to me than the cuddy. (*as before*) Herrin! buy my fat fresh herrin!
(*Girzie exits* R. 1 E.

Hutch. She's a woman with her hands full taking care of a simpleton son, a poor demented being, who has not half the sense of his mother's donkey. But I wonder where's the skipper? Messmates, where's the skipper, Carrach?

Sailor. I saw him up at the Port Inn, a while ago.

Hutch. Stowing away "viskey" as he calls it.

Sailor. Yes, and a nice humor he'll be in when we set sail.

Hutch. Pshaw, mate, Carrach's always soberest when he's drunk —but yonder he comes now.

Enter, Ivan Carrach L. 1 E.

Carrach. Hoo, noo! ye set o' lazy Heilan prutes! are ye re .dy to slip the cable an' set sail?

Hutch. Aye, except Simpson, who says he'll not set sail on Friday.

Car. He pe-tam. Friday or Sunday, it's a' ane, the tides up an' win' favorable. I'll leave to-day if I have to man the ship alone, the superstitious gomerils, pe-tam.

Hutch. Well, skipper, when you're ready, we are.

Car. When I am I'll let you know, so you need na put yoursel' in a fret about it, my man. I'll gang noo and get my papers frae the laird, and see that a' is in ship-shape by the time I come back.

(exit Carrach L. 1 E.

Hutch. Aye, aye, sir.

(busying himself with the rest loading—exeunt L. 3. E.

Enter, Adam Lindsay and Robin Gray, L. 1 E.

Robin. The drunken fuil! That man 'll come tae a bad end some day yet. But Adam, hoo's your daughter?

Adam. As guid in soul an' body as ever, Robin, warkin' awa' like a true daughter for her helpless mither an' mysel'.

Robin. Ah, but she's a fine girl. What a guid wife she'll make some man some day.

Adam. She shows her guid bringing up, an' if any lass deserves a guid home an' husband, it's my Jeannie.

Rob. What for does she no' get married?

Adam. Oh, she's content enough to bide at hame a wee yet. Jeanes Falcon, an' honester chield wha does na' live in the toon, has told his traith to her, but waiting for the laird tae start him in the warld, as he's promised tae do, the lad is no' ready for the hame comin' yet.

Rob. A weel-disposed, weel-spoken lad Jeamie is, but gin he waits till the laird finds it in his heart to give him an ootfit he'll bide a lang while, for a mair selfish, graspin' wretch than Nicol McWhapple does na' draw the breath o' life, gin I'm no mistaken.

Adam. Seein' I hae had a bit o' experience wi' the laird, I winna contradict ye, Robin. But I maun gang after my net to tak' hame an' mend.   *(exit* R. 1 E.

Rob. Sae she's 'trathed to Jeanie! A weel-matched couple they will mak'. Heigh-hum! that's what it is to be young an' strappin. Yet I'm no' sae auld nor sic' a bad lookin' chiel mysel'. A lass micht tak' anither no' sae auld an' fare warse. Bonnie Jeannie, I mind the day she was a wee toddlin' bairn when I dandled her on my knee; but that's a lang time ago, an' since syne she's grown up a shapely woman an' I an old doitered daddy. Daddy? deed I'm no' that, nor likely to be one either.   *(exit* R. 1 E.

Enter, Jeamie and Nicol, L 1 E.

Nicol. (*tapping snuff-box*) Do ye mean to say Jeamie, that I would be guilty of anything dishonorable, or in contravention of the law of the land?

Jeamie. I'm not to say anything, unless you provoke me, laird.

Nic. Well, are you trying to threaten me into submission to your wishes?

Jeam. Threaten? I come to you and tell you I want to get married and you see no objection to that. Then I remind you that you promised to let me have the farm of Askaig some day.

Nicol. I'll say that yet, and I never break my word.

Jeam. Well, I tell you I want it now, and you answer by asking how much money I have to stock it. And when I tell you that I have nothing, you hold up your hands and give me a sermon about extravagance and riotous living.

Nicol. In the which I was but doing my duty as an elder of the church and as your friend.

Jeam. May be so laird, as an elder it might be your duty to preach, but as my friend you knew I never had a chance to be a spendthrift. In return for the work I have given you without a grumble and without a fee, I ask you now to let me have the farm, and give me two years credit for the stock.

Nicol. Which is a very modest demand in your estimation, no doubt.   *(tapping his snuff box)*

Jeam. Modest enough, considering that I have brought a good few hundred into your purse, besides I am going to be married and I must have the means to keep a wife.

Nicol. A very sensible determination Jeamie—I commend your forethought in looking out for the meal before you bring a hungry mouth to the porridge-pot. That's an excellent principle to observe.

Jeam. Thank you for discovering so much good in me, but when you answered me with a lot of texts about ingratitude and self-seeking, I could not help letting you learn that I knew where a part of your money came from.

Nicol. You mean of course, your own suspicions, which are not worth anything in a court o' law. But we'll set that aside for the present, and if you please, we'll talk of your own particular affairs.

Jeam. That's more to my liking.

Nicol. Very well; you have stated your case with as much ability as lawyer Carnegie could have done. Now let me state mine.

Jeam. Out with it.

Nicol. Jeamie, I have been a father to you—you have been treated as if you were my own son, and I'm not saying but that I have had thoughts of making you my heir. But now you come and make a demand upon me, just as though you had a right to, as if you had forgotten you are neither kith nor kin to me.

Jeam. No, laird, I have forgotten nothing.

Nicol. Well, it does no harm to remind you that fifteen years ago a woman with a lad about six years old came to my house. She was foot-sore and hungry, and I took pity on her. I gave her meat and drink and a bed to lay on. People said I ought to have sent her to the poor-house, but I kept her home in charity.

Jeam. Yes, people said, and say, that you had other reasons beside charity for keeping her where nobody could learn what she had to say for herself or her child.

Nicol. Well, she died, and I buried her at my own expense in the churchyard. You know where.

Jeam. *(affected)* Yes, I do, well.

Nicol. Then her boy, who had no friends that any one knew about, would have had to go to the orphan asylum, but I kept him gave him a decent education and bringing up. If he has worked for me it was no more than I had a right to expect after all I had done for him. Lastly, I think that before he speaks of setting up for

himself and asking me for the loan of the necessary capital, he ought
to think of repaying me the outlay I have been to on his account.

Jeam. So be it then. I'll pay you every farthing of it if I live,
but I'll work no more for you. What is the sum you demand in
addition to the work you have already had?

Nicol. I could not just exactly tell you at a moment's notice, but
I'll make up the account.

Jeam. And I'll pay it, if I live. But let there be no more talk of
gratitude between us seeing that I know enough to hang you if I
cared to follow up the clue.   (*going*

Nicol. Stop a little, Jeamie, lad, stop a little. Although you
have lost your temper and consequently your common sense, I still
have mine. You have scarcely a penny in your purse, and yet you
are talking of repaying me may be a hundred pounds—just as though
you had a bag of gold. I'll not press you for your account, but
what are you going to do for a living? Hire yourself out? I'll
give you a recomendation.

Jeam. No, I'll not hire myself out.

Nicol. Maybe you'd like to turn sailor?

Jeam. That is what I mean to do. A sailor has better wages than
a plowman and more chance of making money, and I must make
money.

Nicol. Just so. Then if you like, I'll speak to Ivan Carrach—his
brig is to sail to-night and maybe he'll give you a berth if I ask him.

Jeam. I'll accept this service from you because it 'll help me to
pay your debt the sooner.

Nicol. Very well, I'll go and see the skipper now —(*aside*)— and
I'll double the insurance, then if anything should happen, it's all
through his own stubbornness—and the Lord's will be done.

                                                          (*exit*, R. 1 E.

Jeam. So my foster father will not let me have the Askaig farm!
Never mind, my laird o' Clashgirn; the time may come when you'll
want a favor from me. Well, after all I have no right to expect him
to make any sacrifices on my account—I can work and Jeannie can
wait. Ah, here's her father coming now, and I'll wager she's not
far behind.

                    Enter Adam Lindsay, R. 1 E.

Adam. Well, Jeames, how's all wi' ye?

Jeam. So, so. But where's Jeannie?

Adam. She's comin' yonder—but what's wrong wi' ye, that ye're
scowlin' so.

Jeam. Everything's wrong Adam; but you'll know about it soon
enough. I'll tell it to Jeannie first.

Adam. (*aside*) Somethin's happened atween the lad an' the laird
likely. I'll leave them alone.   (*exit* L. 1 E.

                    Enter Jeannie, R. 1 E.

Jeam. Here you are my sunshine, smiling as usual.

Jean. And what trouble has befel you laddie, that your brow
looks clouded?

Jeam. Well, Jeannie, you must know our marriage must be post-
poned for a year, maybe two years, for the laird has broken his
promise, and I must go to work for money to buy a home to take
you to.

Jean. We're not that old but we can wait a year or two Jeamie, and maybe it's better so, for I do not know what mother would do if I was out of the house.

Jam. Yes, but I had hoped to offer your mother a home with us, and now there's no chance of that for a long while, and the Lord knows what may happen before then. The outlook is a gloomy one for us both.

Jean. But we need not make it worse than it is Jeamie, by frightening ourselves with thoughts of browaies and kelpies that may never come near us. The best way is to take a stout heart to a steep hill, an I as the minister says, 'who knows what fortune we'll find when we get to the top!'

Jam. You're a sensible lass, yet I did not mean to draw a long face nor bewail my lot, but to tell you that the thought of you will put strength into my heart and arms, that for your sake I will work, yes and win, too.

Jean. That's more like yourself Jeamie; but what do you think of doing? Will you fee yourself an't work on a farm?

Jam. No, lassie; I'm tired of farming with the laird, and I have made up my mind to take a voyage where strange sights will make the time pass faster, until I come back and make you my own wife.

Jean. Rest assured, no matter where you are, my thoughts and prayers will be with you. (*Dist—" When ye gang awa' Jeamie."*

Jeam. Now honey, will you not walk a bit down by the water, where we can tell our troth as we have often done to the whispering sea, over which I will soon be sailing?

Jean. Yes, laddie; and after this when I hear it I will think it whispers of you, and my thoughts will go to you across the blue.

(exeunt arm in arm L. 3 E.

Enter Carnegie and Nicol, R. 1 E.

Carnegie. Well laird, here's your insurance papers duly and formally drawn up; but I cannot help expressing my opinion that the insurance is a pretty heavy one for such a light freight. (*gives papers*

Nicol. You are welcome to your opinion lawyer; the cargo is well worth the indemnity I take out for it.

Carnegie. Maybe so; but the company I am agent for, may think differently if they should be called upon to pay it, should anything befall the vessel.

Nicol. They take their risks as well as myself; besides you see, Carrach's bound to set sail to-day.

Carnegie. Does that make it any more dangerous?

Nicol. But it is Friday!

Carnegie. Och, dang the superstition! Every day is a good day; if not what for does the tide rise, the wind blow, and the sun shine?

Nicol. Sure enough. Of course I don't see any difference myself—I merely expressed the common belief among the sailors.

Carnegie. Well, if a man's intentions be good and his work honest and lawful, he has nothing to fear on Friday any more than on any other day. Good day. (*exit* L. 1 E.

Nicol. "If a man's intentions be good, and his work honest and lawful!" I wonder if he suspects what I'm about!

Enter, Ivan Carrach, L. 1 E.

Car. Ah, ye was here! I thought ye were not comin' to let me get away this tide.

Nicol. I have been delayed in getting out the insurance papers; but are you determined to get off to-day?

Car. Aye am I, and pe-tam to the superstitious fuils who'll not sail with me.

Nicol. How many men have you?

Car. Only three beside mysel'.

Nicol. But you cannot work the brig with only yourself and three men.

Car. Oh, I'll just drop into the first port and get all the hands I want. Gie us a pinch frae your mull.   (*reaching for snuff-box*

Enter *Girzie*, slily, R. 3 E.

Girzie. (*aside*) What! The laird and Carrach wi' their heads together? There's mischief afoot I'll warrant. I'll hide and hear what they say.   (*listens*

Nicol. Well, if you had but three hands, would you be more apt to meet with mishaps?

Car. I dinna ken but I might find it difficult to save the ship should I get caught in a storm.

Nicol. Then do not stop and get any more men.

Car. What do ye mean? Oh, I see, ye——

Nicol. (*putting his finger to his lips*) Hus-h, man, you know my meaning and that's enough.

Car. But yer lairdship, my post as skipper?

Nicol. Never mind your place as skipper — should you lose the Colin, I'll get you a faster and better ship; besides here's what'll do away with your fears on that score.   (*gives him money*

Car. Thank ye, that's a' right.

Nicol. And here's your bill of lading.   (*gives it*

Car. Very weel. (*looks at it*) What! Value five hundred poun's—that's——

Nicol. Hush, man! Put it in your pocket.

Car. (*putting it in his pocket*) Oh, aye, now I see!

Nicol. And now my man, you know Jeames Falcon?

Car. Aye, that strappin', saucy lad?

Nicol. Yes. Well, I have found out he knows more about the doings of you and I than would be best to let get out.

Car. What! Apout the smugglin'?

Nicol. Hush, man. Yes. Now he has taken it into his head to go to sea, and I want you to give him a place on the Colin.

Car. Ah, ye want to get him out o' the way?

Nicol. Yes; and I would not cry my eyes out if anything serious happened to him on the voyage.

Car. I take the hint. Let me count the silver. (*aside*) Oom-hoo, my laird! So you wadna care if I should lose the brig an' the lad at the same time, eh? Let's see how much ye pay me for it.

Girzie. (*aside*) A fine elder o' the kirk ye are, ye hypocritical deevil ye! But I'll try and circumvent ye in the hellish plots ye're planning.   (*exit R. 3 E.*

Nicol. (*aside*) If my plans do not work out as I want them to, it will be the fault of the tool and not the planner.

Car. (*having counted the money*) Thank ye, laird, it's a' right.

Nicol. You understand then Carrach, it would be no great loss to you or me, if anything happened the brig—and the lad is trouble-some and might do you harm.

Car. I know all apout it.

Nicol. Od! It's extraordinar'! Here's the lad himself!

Enter, Jeamie, L . 3 E.

Nicol. I have spoken to Carrach, Jeamie, and arranged everything for you with him; but you can speak to him yourself now, and I'll see you when you get through. (*stands apart*

Car. So you be that lad?

Jeam. I suppose so; will I do?

Car. You'll no' be 'fraid to sail on a Friday?

Jeam . No.

Car. Then you'll do; and as I want to clear the port afore twelve if it's possible, shust to spite them gomerils who are 'fraid of the Friday, the sooner you're on board the petter—pe-tam. (*exit* R.

Nicol. (*advancing*) Well, lad, have you engaged yourself to the skipper?

Jeam. Yes, sir; and glad I am of the chance to get away and earn my own living.

Nicol. Od! It's extraordinar'! Well, well, go your own way, Jeamie, lad, but ye'll travel a'day and a night before ye find a home like the one ye leave behind.

Jeam. For what you have done, laird, accept my thanks; for what you might have done—well, I had no right to expect it.

Nicol. Well, I must go, and since you're bound to sail, good-speed and a pleasant voyage, should I not see you again.

Jeam. Thank ye.

Nicol. (*aside*) Od! It's extraordinar'! (*exit* R. 1 E.

Enter, Hutchison, L. 3 E.

Hutch. Are you the lad the skipper shipped for a voyage on the Colin?

Jeam. Yes, mate; my name's Jeames Falcon, and well met am I with such a good-hearted mess-mate as I know you to be.

Hutch. Thank you. Here's my hand, and may we sail many a voyage together—but the skipper's waiting for you.

Jeam. Is he? I'm loth to delay him, but you see I'm expecting my lass down with a few clothes I want to take with me.

Hutch. Then come as quick as you can, for the skipper is in no very good humor at being kept waiting—and a caution for friendship's sake—bear yourself as evenly as possible————

Jeam. What do you mean?

Hutch. You see the rest of the crew saw you talking with the laird just now, and I fear they take it ill.

Jeam. Ill! How, man?

Hutch. To speak plain, they suspicion you.

Jeam. Suspicion me of what?

Hutch. Of being a spy.

Jeam. Why should they think that—I have given them no cause?

Hutch. Maybe not, but they know you're a friend of the owner, and have an idea that you may tell of any ongoings that might not be according to rule.

Jeam. What, me? If they only knew how little friendship there is between the laird and me, they would soon get rid of that idea.

Hutch. I'm glad to hear you say't. Come aboard as quick as you can. (*exit,* L. 3 E.

Enter, Girzie, R. 1 E.

Girzie. There's the chiel alone now—I'll speak to him and warn him in time.

Jeam. Hallo! Who's that?

Girzie. 'Deed, and it's just me, Girzie Todd, and I hae' been lookin' for ye.

Jeam. Looking for me? What for, Girzie?

Girzie. Adam Lindsay told me ye were to sail in the Colin.

Jeam. And so I am; I'm going on board now, as she sails to-night. What then?

Girzie. I wanted to warn you no' to gang wi' Ivan Carrach.

Jeam. And why not?

Girzie. Ye'll maybe think it an old wife's notion, but listen—ye want to come back and marry Jeannie, and ye'll never come back if ye gang in that boat.

Jeam. Pshaw, Girzie, why should I not go in the Colin as well as any other?

Girzie. Because the Colin is *doomed!*

Jeam. How do you happen to know all this?

Girzie. I canna' tell any more, and if it hadna' been for Jeannie's sake, I wouldna' have said as muckle. But gang ye in the Colin, and ye'll never be guidman to Jeannie Lindsay.

Jeam. If any danger threatens the brig, that's all the more reason why I should be aboard, for if I can save her, it'll maybe repay some of the debt I owe Clashgirn.

Girzie. Have yer way. I have done all I can to save ye.

(exit R. 3 E.

Jeam. What's got into the Fishwife's head? She's surely been drinking, or is uncanny! Ah, here comes my lass!

Enter, Jeannie, R. 1 E.

Jeam. Well, sweetheart, you have come at last?

Jean. Yes, laddie. I'm sorry I kept you waiting so long, but besides getting your clothes, I had to see to mother a bit, who's worse to-day.

Jeam. I am sorry to hear it, but take heart Jeannie. I have but a crown, and to make that crown a pound, I am going away to sea and when I return I'll make things easier for your folks as well as yourself.

Jean. We will live in hope and trust to Providence.

Jeam. Now lassie, I must leave you; the anchor is weighed and I must go, but it's a heavy heart I leave behind.

Jean. Cheer up, I'll keep your heart warm in my bosom until you return to give me your hand in exchange.

Jeam. Lord love and bless you, lass, for those words; they will ring in my ears when I am far away.

Jean. One last embrace, Jeamie. *(they embrace*

Jeam. Lord, lassie, how your heart thumps!

Jean. Yes, leaping with love, and throbbing with pain at the thought of parting.

Jean. If it grieves you so much, I'll not go away.

Jean. Say not that, but go the way Providence or fate has set before you.

Jeam. One more kiss, the last alone, my lass, for yonder some folks are coming.

Jean. My father, Robin Gray, Wattie and others, come to see you off.

Enter, Adam Lindsay, Robin Gray, Monduff, Carnegie, Wattie and Nicol, L. 1 E.

Jeam. Well met, friends, and thank you for the friendly part of coming to see me off.

Robin. It's nae mair nor a neighbor's duty, Jeamie.

Adam. Aye, lad, and well I ken you will be missed by one at any rate.

Jeam. If there's one misses me when I'm gone, I'll be sure of one welcome when I come back.

Robin. Ye'll be sure o' mair than one welcome, for a' yer friends 'll be glad to greet ye, my lad.

Adam. My lass here, will miss ye in the long gloamin', when the work is done, an' she sits by the door alone.

Jean. Yes, father, that will I, but looking over the sea, my heart will be with Jeamie, my own true love.			(*sobbing.*

Robin. But if it grieves ye so, lass, what for will the lad leave ye?

Jeam. To earn some money, Robin, to buy her a home.

Robin. I thought the laird here, was bounden to gie ye a start. How is this, Clashgirn? What for will ye let Jeamie leave to get a livin', when he's been dependin' and lookin' to you for't?

Nicol. The lad must wait till times are better and money not scarce, when I will give him the Askaig place as I promised, but if he will sow his wild oats abroad, why he may then for all me.

Robin. Weel, Jeamie, if that's a' what's wantin' to keep ye at home, for your lassie's sake I'll start ye wi' stock an' house wi' my own silver, an' not let ye be beholden to any laird.

Nicol. Od! It's extraordinar' that every one thinks a laird's purse is never empty!

Jeam. Thank you, Robin, for your friendly offer, but as a man, well in body, I cannot accept it. My lass must wait till I return with enough of my own earnings to get a farm, when we'll settle down, well off and content.

Jean. And willing am I to wait till then, my lad.

Adam. An' as her father, I'll no' see her want.

Robin. Nor will I as her auld friend an' neighbor.

Jeam. Well, leaving her in such good hands, I bid you all farewell.			(*shaking hands.*

Robin. Farewell, Jeamie, an' a pleasant voyage.

Adam. God speed ye laddie, wi' the best o' success.

Carnegie. A safe passage and quick return.

Monduff. The Lord prosper you James, in the strange path that lies before you. Before you go, accept of this bible — read it constantly, and remember that you are as safe on the sea as on land, when you are in God's care.			(*presenting book.*

Jeam. Thank you.

Nicol. (*offering his hand*) Good bye, Jeames.

Jeam. Well, I don't know—but there.			(*they shake hands.*

Nicol. (*aside*) Od! It's extraordinar'!			(*takes snuff.*

Wattie. What for are ye all cryin'?

Robin. Toots, ye fuil, dinna ye see that **friend Jeamie's going away**?

Wattie. Are you not goin' to take me?

Jeam. Not this time.

Wattie. Will you the next?

Jeam. I will not promise, but I'll see. Now, farewell my lass.
Jean. Farewell, my lad, a fond farewell.

He embraces her and is about to go on board, when Girzie steps out from behind a bale and stops him.

Girzie. Hold, I tell ye! Gang ye not on the Colin, or sadly ye'll rue it.
Adam. Girzie, what do ye mean?
Robin. The auld wife is surely daft.
Nicol. No, she's superstitious, and fears for the fate of the Colin if it sails to-day—Friday.
Robin. Ha, ha, ha! That's it!
Girzie. Weel, hae your own way, an' rue the day.

Jeamie steps on board and stands throwing a kiss to Jeannie who faints, supported by her father. The rest wave their hats, Girzie shaking her fist threatningly in the laird's face. TABLEAU—The Ship's Departure.

END OF ACT FIRST.

ACT II.

SCENE FIRST.—Interior of Adam's cottage. White bare walls in the centre of the background; window L. C.; practical door R. C.; curtained bed built in wall R.; door L.; table C.; lounge L.; easy chair R. Stage dark—Tableau of Ship on Fire seen through transparent back wall. Mrs. Lindsay discovered in bed asleep, and Jeannie in a troubled sleep on the lounge, as the dream fades and the light dawns.

Jean. (*in her sleep*) Woe is me! Woe is me!
Adam. (*without,* L.) Jeannie! Jeannie!
Jean. (*starting*) Oh, heaven! who called me? Such a fearful dream!
Adam. Jeannie, daughter, do you no' hear me?
Jean. Is that you, father?
Adam. Aye. Bring me a drink o' water, I'm so dry and feverish.
Jean. Yes, father, wait a minute and I'll bring you a cup of milk fresh from the cow. (*exit* D.

Enter Adam, L. *with his arm in a sling.*

Adam. Are ye wauken, wife? (*waking her.*
Mrs L. (*sitting up*) Is that you, guidman?
Adam. Aye, an' no better to-day, confoun' the luck.
Mrs L. Since it be the will o' the Lord, bear it man with christian humility and fortitude.
Adam. It's weel enough to talk, but how can ye expect a man not to complain who's owin' rent an' not able to work, with naebody to depend on but a frail daughter?
Mrs L. Thank God we have her, Adam, to sustain and help us, now that we are not able to help ourselves.
Aaam. What's keepin' her?

Enter Jeannie at door, L.

Well, lass, have ye brought me a drink o' milk?

Jean. Not yet, father — I went to get you some but found Crummie gone.

Adam. Gone! Gone where?

Jean. I do not know; I hunted down the road, thinking she had got loose from tether and had gone to graze, but I could not see her, and I fear she has been taken away.

Adam. Ta'en awa'! Ta'en awa'! How could anybody take her awa'? She is no' a wee thing to be crammed into a tinker's pocket.

Jean. No, father; but they may have driven her away while the storm was blowing so loud that we heard no disturbance.

Adam. The cow stolen awa'! It's no' possible! Ye were surely careless and did not tie her well last night.

Jean. I did, father, as I always do.

Adam. How could she get awa' then? Ow! it does seem as though ruin was bound to come on me in my auld age.

Enter, Monduff at practical door, with basket.

Mon. Why, Adam, what is the use of bewailing your fate that way? Cheer up, man—you'll be able to go about your work in a day or two.

Adam. It's not my broken arm I'm bewailing—it's my stolen cow.

Mon. Your stolen cow!

Adam. Yes, Crummie has been stolen awa' by the tinker gypsies.

Mon. The barefaced rascals!

Adam. Yes, and the cow was the only thing left to gie us a bite an' a sup.

Mrs L. The Lord's will be done.

Mon. That's right Mrs. Lindsay; bear your burden meekly. But here's a lump of ham, and some eggs for you. (*gives them.*

Mrs L. Thank you for your kindness.

Mon. And you, man, hold up your head and do not groan so, for since you're not able to go yourself, I'll go and see if I can find the cow or catch the thief.

Adam. He should be hanged for robbin' a poor man like me.

Mon. And you, lass, stop your crying and get your mother some breakfast. (*Song*—"*The Woefu' Heart.*"

Jean. Very well, sir, I will. (*exit Monduff at* P. D.

Adam. Come here, Jeannie—I didna' mean to speak harsh to ye, but what with yer mither sick, mysel' disabled frae work, and the cow stolen awa'—it's enough to make any man lose his temper.

Jean. Say no more about it, father. With the help of God, we'll bear up till Jeannie comes home, then we'll all live in our own house together with plenty.

Adam. Yes, but who's to pay the rent that's owin', and will be due the laird afore then?

Jean. Trust to Providence. Come, mother.

Mrs L. Yes, the Lord's will be done. (*exit Jeannie and Mrs. L.* L.

Enter Robin Gray, P. D.

Robin. Weel Adam, I hae brought a bottle o' guid French brandy for ye—an' how are ye to-day?

Adam. Fairly, thank ye—that is, as weel as can be expected in a man as sorely troubled as I am, an' not able to work. I fear me it'll be a while afore I get the use o' my arm.

Robin. But ye're gettin' on bravely for a' that, an' ye'll be a' right in time.

Adam. Ah, in time, no doubt! But Lord knows what we're to do, biding that time.

Robin. Here, hae a dram—(*giving him a drink*)   But what's wrong, man! What's wrong?

Adam. Everything's wrong—our cow's been stolen.

Robin. Your cow stolen awa'?

Adam. Yes, an' the auld wife's gettin' worse and worse, an' mysel' in this condition, and Jeannie wrought clean off her feet without making any better o't. Is no' that enough to make a man who was askin' no one a penny till now, as sour as a crab apple? An' to back it a', there's the laird hirplin here day after day about his rent, an' no way that I know to pacify him.

Robin. An' ye're owin' him rent?

Adam. Aye. The fishin's been so poor o' late, I hae fell behind wi' Clashgirn, whom I'm expectin' this very hour.

Robin. Hoots, man! why did you not let me know that afore? I could ha' set your mind at rest without any trouble.

Adam. I know that, but Jeannie an' her mither was bidding me bear my own burden—and I never cared mysel' to be beholden to anybody.

Robin. Aye, but ye'll except me, Adam. Say nothing about it, an' I'll settle wi' the laird, though I'd rather deal wi' anybody but him since we had that dispute about the line fence.

Adam. Thank ye, Carnieford. If ye'll oblige me, I'll be able to pay ye back ———

Robin. We'll talk about that again. Hark! A horse's tramp! The laird's comin' now. Gang in the tither room, an' I'll meet an' settle wi' the man, though I had as soon dicker with the de'il.

Adam. Weel, just as you say.   (*exit,* L.

Enter, *Girzie,* R.

Girzie. (*at the door*) Watty, gie the cuddy his peck o' meal, an' eat the piece that's in the pouch yersel'.

Robin. (*aside*) It's no' the laird—it's the fishwife.

Girzie. Some fine fresh herrin' the day, Mrs. Lindsay? Hallo! you here? Where's the folks, Mr. Robin?

Robin. In the hoose at their breakfast?

Girzie. An' how are they, to-day?

Robin. Not very happy, seein' their cow has been stolen awa'.

Girzie. God help them. Then it's too true that misfortunes never come single.

Robin. (*going*) Aye, but I must say good day to ye.

Girzie. Bide a wee, Carnieford, there's ill news come home this fine mornin' for some folks ye care about.

Robin. What news, good woman?

Girzie. The news is that the Colin's been burned at sea, and Jeames Falcon has been drowned or burned wi' her.

Robin. Heaven save us, woman, what are ye sayin'?

Girzie. What's true, I'm thinkin'. Ivan Carrach landed here this mornin' wi' the news, an' he's up at the laird's now.

Robin. But—are ye sure that Falcon is dead?

Girzie. Ask the laird.

Robin. But how do you ken this?

Girzie. Nae matter—ask the laird and Carrach if it is no' true, and then ye can tell Jeannie.

Robin. No, Girzie, I canna' do that! But you are a friend to both her an' me—gang in yersel' an' tell her, if you're sure it's true.

I will see the laird and Carrach, since yonder they're comin'. But break it to her kindly.

Girzie. I'll do your bidding for the sake o' the kind word and bag o' meal ye had for my Wattie. Dinna fear for Jeannie, she is young an' hearty, an' she'll get over this afore long, and it's an ill wind that fills naebody's sails, even though there's a smell o' brimstone intill't. (*exit,* L. D.

Enter, Nicol and Carrach, P. D.

Nicol. Hallo! Cairnieford, is that you? I'm glad to see you.

Robin. I canna' say the same for you.

Nicol. Well, well, you need not be so cross. I thought you were to let bygones be bygones.

Robin. Bygones are bygones wi' me, so far that I hae no thoughts o' bringin' them up.

Nicol. Where are the folks of the house?

Robin. Where in their trouble they dinna' wish to be fashed by you. I suppose ye hae come after Adam Lindsay's rent?

Nicol. Yes, six pounds he is owing me.

Robin. Well, here, I am ready to pay it, and when you hae given me a quittal, I hae a question to ask you.

Nicol. Od! It's quite extraordinar'! And so you are going to pay Adam Lindsay's rent? Well, Adam is an honest man, and he's got a bonnie daughter.

Robin. That's neither here nor there—here's your money in notes—count them.

Nicol. They're right, no doubt—(*looking them over*)—and here is the receipt. *gives it.* But you were saying there was a question—

Robin. Aye. I want to ken if it is true that the Colin has been lost, and Jeames Falcon has gone down wi' her?

Nicol. It is true, though who told you I cannot guess, as I was the first to know it a few hours since. The brig was one of the best that ever sailed, but she was burned, and my poor young friend who was trying to save the papers and log, was either killed by the explosion of a barrel of gunpowder, or drowned. Is not that the way of it, Carrach?

Car. Aye. He was a prave lad, but the 'splosion was too strong for him—pe-tam.

Robin. And hoo muckle did you gain by it, Mister Nicol?

Nicol. I? I was the one who lost by the accident.

Robin. So you say; but you ken and I ken, Nicol McWhapple, there are reasons why I should doubt your word—especially when it concerns Jeames Falcon. (*exit,* P. D.

Nicol. Od! It's extraordinar!

Car. Aye! It was—pe-tam!

Enter, Carnegie, P. D.

Carnegie. Hallo, McWhapple; you here?

Nicol. Yes, it is myself. Have you heard from the company yet?

Carnegie. Yes, I have just heard from them.

Nicol. And they found the policy, and the affidavits of the crew all right?

Carnegie. Satisfactory, with the exception of the lacking presence of the mate, Hutchison.

Nicol. Of course they must find fault with something. Well I should like a settlement as soon as possible. Come, Carrach, let us go.

Carnegie. By the way, did you hear? The coast guards say there has been a heap of smugglin' hereabout?

Car. Eh! What's that?

Nicol. Smugglin's an awful ruination to honest traders.

Carnegie. You do a little in the brandy and tobacco line, don't you?

Nicol. Yes, at times.

Carnegie. Then you'll be glad to know that the guagers are on the track of the smugglers, and are determined to put them down.

Nicol. A good thing for honest trade—a good thing! Good day to you, Carnegie.

Carnegie. Good day.

Car. (*aside*) Bad day to ye, and—pe-tam!

(*exit, Nicol and Carrach,* P. D.

Carnegie. He winced when I give him a dab. Now I'll go in and see how Adam and his family are getting along.   (*exit,* L. D.

Enter, Girzie and Jeannie, L. D.

Jean. Drowned? Drowned?

Girzie. Aye, lassie.

Jean. How can I bear it? How can I bear it?

Girzie. Just like other folks. It is hard to think of it at first, but it's wonderful how one's sorrow softens after a day or two, when a thing is past help.

Jean. But it cannot—it cannot be true!

Girzie. I would say 'it cannot be true' if it would do any good to tell a lie, but it would be a lie, an' you'd be so much the worse for it afterwards.

Jean. But there was no one saw him go down?

Girzie. But there was no one saw him come up, either. Ye need no' be deceiving yoursel' for expecting miracles. I have had more sorrow hoping for what was impossible, than I ever had from real misfortune.

Jean. Drowned, drowned! My Jeamie drowned, and me thinking day and night of him coming home to save us from all our troubles. Had it not been for that, I would not have been able to bear up at all, and now——   (*throws herself on her knees, and buries her face in the bed, sobbing bitterly.*)

Girzie. Toots, Jeannie! Do not take on so—it will not bring him back. Cheer up, and do your duty by the auld folks, and remember there's as good fish in the sea as ever came out o't, whatever one may think of their last fishin'.   (*about to go.*

Jean. O, woe is me! O, woe is me!

Enter, Robin Gray and Wattie, P. D.

Girzie. Well, Cairnieford, the blow has been struck, and it's no' with pleasure I did it. Poor lass!

Wattie. What for is Jeannie cryin', mother?

Girzie. Because Jeannie Falcon is drooned.

Wattie. Drooned! Where?

Girzie. At the bottom of the sea—he's dead, we'll never see him again.   (*going.*

Robin. Well, Girzie, an' must ye be off?

Girzie. Aye, I hae my day's work afore me yet. (*aside to Robin*) I would no' say much about it to Jeannie, she's takin' it sore to heart.

(*exit with Wattie,* P. D.

Robin. Poor lass! I feel so sorry for her, and fain would comfort her.

Jean. Jeamie drowned! It cannot be!

Robin. It's too true, lassie.

Jean. Is it you, Mr. Gray? *(rising.*

Robin. Aye. I brought ye a few things I thought ye might need.

Jean. You are placing us under new obligations every day. *(wiping her eyes and taking basket)* And now I do not think we shall ever be able to pay you back.

Robin. Dinna speak o' that. An' here's a bottle of medicine the doctor gave me for your father. *(handing her a bottle.*

Jean. Ah, poor father! What a sad lookout there is for him now that all my bright prospects are dashed away. O, woe is me!

Robin. Dinna allow yourself to be carried away wi' grief for the dead—think o' the livin'—your father and mither, who need your dutiful care.

Jean. *(drying her eyes)* That is so. Thank you for your friendly words—I have nothing now to live for but to care for my parents.

Robin. Aye—an' here's a bottle o' wine for your mither—an' how is she now?

Jean. Better, and she's fallen asleep now.

Robin. That's weel—and—and Jeannie, there's something I have wanted to say to ye a long time.

Jean. What is it, Mr. Gray?

Robin. I want ye to marry me, Jeannie.

Jean. Oh, no, you do not!

Robin. It's the plain truth, an' that's the way ye can relieve yoursel' o' all the weight o' debt ye fancy ye are owin' me.

Jean. Woe is me! Woe is me!

Robin. I'm an auld man may be for such a young lass, but ye would no' find any difference in me as long as I live. I'll try to make you happy, lass, and your father and mither comfortable. That's all I hae to say.

Jean. You have been a good friend to us at our sorest need, and if you had asked me to lay down my life for you, I would have done it willingly; but I cannot, cannot, be your wife when I think of him that's away.

Robin. Ye cannot be his now, or I would no' hae spoken. But ye can if ye will, mak' three folk happy—for their sakes Jeannie, dinna refuse me.

Jean. I know that he is away, but my thoughts are with him yet, and I could not be a true wife always thinking of him. There is nothing for me to do now, but to help my father and mother.

Robin. Ye'll do that best as mistress o' Cairnieford, an' your memory o' Jeames Falcon will no' mak' ye a bit worse a wife.

Jean. Give me a while to think—I cannot answer you now.

Robin. May be I should no' hae spoken yet, but it's been hard work to keep the upper hand o' the thoughts that hae been running through my head. Jeannie, ye hae been like the light o' heaven to me. God forgive me if it be wrong to feel so.

Jean. Oh, do not say any more!

Robin. I must speak out now, if it was the last time I was ever to speak to ye. I ken how ridiculous it is for a man like me to be speakin' that way, but dinna ye laugh at me, for that would drive me mad—though may be I deserve it.

Jean. Heaven knows how I wish I could give you such a heart as you deserve.

Robin. Those were sweet words to one that never knew what it was to hae anybody to love him for his own sake. Ye need no' draw from me, Jeannie—powerful though this passion be, it has no' the power to mak' me forget that I am Robin Gray, two score an' ten, an' ye are a young lassie whose kind heart pities me, but can do no more.

Jean.   I would do anything in the world but that to please you.

Robin.   And this is the only thing in the world that can please me. If ye will come to my home and bring the sunshine into it, ye will never have cause to sorrow, if it be in the power o' mortal man to mak' ye happy.

Jean.   I have no doubt of that.

Robin.   An' ye will promise to be the guidwife o' Cairnieford?

Enter, Adam suddenly, L. D.

Adam.   Aye, an' ye will hae my good will to it.

Robin.   Thank ye, Adam, but it is the lassie's I want first.

Adam.   Ye'll hae that, Cairnieford, ye'll hae that. Go into the room a while wi' the guidwife.

Robin.   Very well.   *(exit,* L. D.

Adam.   Well, what answer are ye going to give Cairnieford?

Jean.   O, woe is me! O, woe is me!

Adam.   What's wrong, lass? Do ye not hear what I am sayin'?

Jean.   Yes, father, I hear you.

Adam.   What for did ye no' speak then?

Jean.   I was going to speak, father, if you had given me time. I have been thinking of it, and—and——

Adam.   Weel, what are ye hirplin' at now?

Jean.   I do not think I ought—I do not think I can.

Adam.   What? Dinna think ye can marry him? Is he no' a weel doing man, an' a kind hearted man, an' all that any sensible woman would desire?

Jean.   He is all that you say, and more, but I cannot marry him, or anybody.

Adam.   An' what for, no?

Jean.   For the reason I gave him—I am not fit to be any man's wife with all my heart lying out yonder with Jeanie in the sea.

Adam.   Ye canna' marry a drooned man can ye? Ye will no' get such another chance as Cairnieford's this twelvemonth and more.

Jean.   I do not want an offer, father—I do not want to marry.

Adam.   You would drive a saint out o' his wits wi' anger. A nice thing for a man come to my years, that has wrought hard a' my days to gie ye a decent up-bringin', to find that my own daughter winna do my biddin'.

Jean.   I never refused to do your bidding before, father, and I would not now, but I cannot help it.

Adam.   Why? Do ye no' like the man?

Jean.   Yes.

Adam.   Then what was it? Was it because ye just wanted to anger me? Ye will be nae daughter o' mine if ye dinna tell Cairnieford that ye will tak' him and be thankfu'.

Jean.   O, woe is me! O, woe is me!

Adam.   It's the most extraordinary nonsense I ever heard tell of, to think that ye hae your face against me and your mither, and a man like Cairnieford, and for no other reason than that the man ye wanted is drooned. Now hear me; I lay my commands upon ye to answer Cairnieford as I want ye to, an' if ye don't, ye'll be the sufferer. And as for me and your mither, we are not long for this world now, but I didna' expect that our last days were to be made miserable by the disobedience of our only child.

Jean. O, woe is me! O, woe is me!

Adam. I'll gang and send Robin in—and remember your duty as my daughter. (*exit,* L. D.

Jean. My duty! O, God, show me the right way, for I do not wish to turn aside from the path of duty. O, woe is me! Woe is me!

Enter, Robin, L. D.

Robin. (*aside*) Yonder she is, poor soul! I have half a mind to to gie it up, yet what will breome o' her and her helpless folk! Jeannie, lassie, I am waiting for my answer.

Jean. You wish to know what I have determined on?

Robin. There is no use concealing it, Jeannie — I hae poor patience when I'm set on anything, till I ken the best or worst o't—and the hope and fear o' your answer has put me in such a state as is no' pleasant to be kept waiting in.

Jean. I'll not keep you waiting long. I have made up my mind to tell you the truth, and let you decide for yourself.

Robin. The truth! What about?

Jean. About myself. You know all about Jeamie, and you have said it would make no difference. That is another reason for the honor and respect I bear you, besides what you have done for me and mine. But I cannot care for you as I cared for him, and if I was alone, I would say 'no' to your offer, because I honor you and think you should have a wife deserving of you.

Robin. But what better would it be if I did not care for her?

Jean. I cannot answer that. But I was going to say that I am not alone, and for the sake of them that need my help, for the sake of all we are owing you, I'll be your wife, and I'll try to be a faithful one.

Robin. It's a bargain! (*grasping her hand and kissing her*) And that's the earnest.

Jean. You will not heed my being a little quiet—it is more in my heart to weep than smile.

Robin. I'll no' heed anything ye like to do. Bless ye, lassie, ye hae given me a happiness I never ken'd before — I've half a mind to gie ye two or three steps o' the Highland Fling this minute, to relieve mysel' of the joy that's swellin' in my breast. (*dancing.*

Jean. I hope you may never have cause to repent of your joy.

Robin. Nae fear of that—it's new life ye hae given me.

Jean. I shall be glad to see you happy, Robin.

Robin. Then ye'll always be happy, Jennie, lass, for I'll always be happy.

Jean. (*starting and listening eagerly*) Hark! Who is that calling me?

Robin. Naebody, lassie, that I hear.

Jean. (*dazed*) There! Do you not hear?

Robin. What? What, Jeannie!

Jean. Jeamie, calling me.

Robin. Ye're delirious, lassie—your brain is overcome wi' the heap of trouble. Come, nestle your head here, lass, on my bosom. (*drawing her upon his lap.*

Jean. Yes, yes! O, woe is me! O, woe is me!

Robin. Grieve not, lassie—your troubles are at an end noo!

Jean. Yes, yes! O, woe is me! O, woe is me! But yonder he is reaching out his hands for me to come. (*pointing vaguely.*

Robin. You are crazed, lass—keep quiet. (*patting her.*

Adam. (*appearing at the door*) There they are, as loving as two doves. Lord bless ye, my bairn, and mak' this the first o' many happy days.

Girzie. (*appearing at the back door*) Dearie me! She's on with the new love very soon after being off with the auld.

Jean. (*starting up*) Jeanie! Jeanie! I come! (*reaching out as if to embrace her lover, and fainting*)

TABLEAU.—Stage dark, and Jeanie seen through the wall at back, at sea afloat upon a mast.

END OF ACT SECOND.

ACT III.

SCENE FIRST.—The Brownie's Bite. A bridge over a deep gulf in the background. The Fishwife's cot exposed to the left foreground; bushes to the right. Door at the left of cottage, and practical door at back. Wattie discovered on his knees before a smouldring fire.

Enter, Jeamie, R.

Jeam. Yonder is Girzie's cottage.

Wattie. Phew! Phew! Such a heap o' breath it takes to start a little blaze. (*Jeamie opens the back door and stands looking in. Wattie stares at him*) My Lord! Who's you?

Jeam. Well, Wattie, what are you staring at? Do you not know me? Where's your mother?

Wattie. (*rushing to side door*) Mither! Mither, come here!

Enter, Girzie, L. D.

Girzie. (*not seeing Jeamie*) Ye daft idiot, what's wrong that ye call me that way?

Wattie. It's—it's him!

Girzie. Who's him?

Wattie. Him, come up from 'mong the fishes—an' ye said we'd never see him any more—an' it is just a ghost.

Girzie. Who?

Wattie. (*pointing to Jeamie*) Yon wraith.

Jeamie. How are ye, Girzie?

Girzie. Heaven keep an' save us all! Is it yer own self Jeames Falcon?

Jeam. Yes, my own self; who else would it be?

Girzie. Then ye're not drooned?

Jeam. I think not, though I was near enough to it.

Wattie. An' ye have not been biding with the fishes all this time?

Jeam. No, Wattie, I have been living with folks like ourselves.

Wattie. An' what made them tell the lie about ye, having Jeannie crying and sobbing so?

Jeam. Because they thought it true no doubt, and maybe wished it so. And that reminds me of what I came here to ask Girzie.

Girzie. (*aside*) I'll not tell him as long as I can help it. (*aloud*) No, lad, ye'll ask no questions till ye hae had a bite to eat. (*to Wattie*) Run away an' bring in the tatics an' herrin', Wattie. (*Wattie goes out and returns with supper*) Sit ye down there Jeames Falcon, an' tell us how ye got home again. (*gives chair*

Jeam. Thank ye, Girzie.

Girzie. Have ye seen anyone since ye came back?

Jeam. I came around by Adam Lindsay's, but the house was shut up.

Girzie. Aye! An' when did ye come back?

Jeam. I landed at Ayr yesterday, and walked over. I have not been in Portlappoch yet.

Girzie. Then ye hae not heard ought of your friends?

Jeam. Not a word, and that's what brought me here?

Girzie. Just that. But you have no' said a word aboot how ye came to be alive at all. Carrach an' the rest o' them, barrin' Hutchison, came home, and a' said ye were drooned.

Wattie. Aye, tell us how ye were drooned.

Girzie. How did ye escape after the explosion?

Jeam. Finding myself in the water I floated about on a mast for thirty hours, till picked up by a king's ship, on which I was forced to take passage for a year. Well, to finish, after a year's cruise, I landed at Ayr yesterday, and here I am. Now for your news.

Girzie. Draw up your stool an' eat something. (*he draws up stool*) Have no' ye heard aught o' what was going on here?

Jeam. Not a word, I wrote to Jeannie from Malta, but I did not even here if she got the letter; but how is she?

Girzie. Take a bit o' bannock, man and make yerself at home.
(*reaching him the cakes.*)

Wattie. An' did ye not gang down among the fishes?

Jeam. No, Wattie, or you would not have seen me here to-day. Now, Girzie, you know what I am most anxious to hear—how is Jeannie, and where is she?

Girzie. She's well enough for that matter, an' she's at Cairnieford.

Jeam. At Cairnieford! Has she gone into service?

Girzie. Aye, in a kind of a way.

Jeam. Has anything happened to Adam or his wife?

Girzie. They're both livin' yet, and at Cairnieford. Adam met wi' an accident an' broke his arm, but he's most weel again. Mrs. Lindsay's worse nor she was afore, an' is not thought to live long.

Jeam. Poor Jeannie, she must have had a hard time of it.

Girzie. Hard enough, when she did not know where to get bit or sup if it had not een for Robin Gray.

Jeam. The Lord be praised that they had a friend able and willing to help them. Heaven prosper him for it, and he shall not lose anything by it if I live. I'll away to them at once. I cannot rest till I see them, and I'm almost as anxious to get a grip of Cairnie's hand as I am to see Jeannie and get her welcome home.

Girzie. You should not gang up to-night—it'll be late, an' it's not just fair not to gie them warning o' your coming.

Jeam. Why, they'll be all the more delighted at the surprise.

Girzie. I'm not so sure. Ye dinna ken what changes take place after one's dead an' buried as ye have been, for a year.

Jeam. What are you hinting at?

Girzie. Do ye mind what I told ye before ye went awa'?

Jeam. Yes; you wanted me not to sail in the Colin.

Girzie. An' I said if ye did, ye would never be guidman to Jeannie Lindsay. I did no' expect my words to come true in the way they have, but true ye'll find them.

Jeam. In God's name, what is wrong?

Girzie. Well, I suppose ye might as well hear it from me as any other body, so I'll tell ye myself—Jeannie is married.

Jeam. (*staggering and holding his hand to his heart*) Married! Jeannie married! To whom?

Girzie. Him who was her best friend when she thought ye were dead—Cairnieford himself.

Jeam. What! A man old enough to be her father! When did it happen?

Girzie. At the end o' the harvest.

Jeam. So soon! Would to heaven I had been drowned rather than come back to learn this. She was not grieved when I went away, and no doubt she was glad to hear that I could never come back, and was ready to believe it.

Girzie. What was the lassie to do? It would not hae brought ye to life to let her father and mither starve, and herself pine awa' to the kirkyard. If there's anyone to blame, it's yerself for going awa' to foreign parts, an' not letting us know whether ye were living or dead.

Jeam. Oh, Jeannie, woman! Little did I think ye would play me false! (*throws himself into a chair and moans.*

Wattie. What for is Jeamie cryin' mither? Is Jeamie drooned and gone to bide wi' the fishes?

Girzie. Hech, noo'! He is sore taken up about it, and there's no saying what he might do. (*looking out*) Lord save us! There she is coming! I'll gang wi' Wattie out of the way, and leave them to theirselves, poor things. Come, Wattie. (*exit with Wattie,* L. D.

Jeam. Oh, Jeannie, woman! Jeannie, woman!

Enter, Jeannie, R. U. E. *into the cot.*

Jean. (*at the door*) I called, Girzie, to see if you had a nice fat haddock to boil for the good man's supper? (*coming in, she sees Jeamie, who looks up*) Who's that? Oh! Oh-o-h!

(*shrieks and falls upon the floor.*

Jeam. [*partly lifting her*] My Jeannie!

Jean. [*sitting partly up*] Oh! Who are you?

Jeam. Do you not know me?

Jean. Yes, yes, but do not touch me. [*shuddering.*

Jeam. I have come back, Jeannie, to find that you shudder at my touch. And yet it was you, who not very long since, clasped your arms around me, and told me that you would bide my return faithfully. Have you kept your word?

Jean. They told me you were drowned, and my heart was sore to think of it. But you made no sign that you were living, and every one spoke as if there could be no doubt that you were dead. There was no one to whisper a word of hope, and what could I do but believe when the proof was so strong?

Jeam. You could have waited a little for confirmation of the news. Oh, woman! woman! I would have waited a hundred years before I would have cast you so utterly from my breast, and taken another in my arms.

Jean. And I would have waited forevever had I been alone. But they pressed me sore from all sides. I was sad, sad and heart broken—I did not care what became of myself, but I thought it a sin to turn away from the duty before me, and I thought that you, looking at me from the other world, would see what feelings moved me, and would say 'well done.' That was why I married, though my heart was with you. (*with emotion.*

Jeam. Jeannie, Jeannie! you are mine yet—you shall be, in spite of all the marriages on earth. What power has a minister's prayers to part our lives—to fill the years that are before us with lingering misery? It shall have none. You are mine, Jeannie, my own, and no one else has a right to claim you. Rise up then, and come away from this place, and in another country we'll find a home and happiness.

Jean. [*spurning him*] Away, man, away! [*rising*] That's not Jeames Falcon who has risen from the dead, for he would have pitied me, and tried to strengthen me for the cruel duty I must do. It's the evil one himself in my poor lad's body, come to tempt me to my shame.

Jeam. Lord help me! I believe I'm crazed. My brain has been in a whirl since I learned that you were married, and I scarcely know what I do, or say, or think. But I'm not the villain you might think me from what I have said; it was the bad spirit that came between us, made me say the villainous thought—forgive me.

(*kneeling and taking both her hands.*

Jean. I do, but now, go away.

Jeam. I will.   (*kissing her hands.*

Jean. (*drawing them away*) Do not do that—it frightens me, and makes me think of what you said. I cannot bear to think of that, because it would make the sorrow I have to bear all the sorer, if I had to think of you as one who would do a wrong act.

Jeam. No man shall ever say I wronged him.

Jean. You are speaking like yourself now, and it comforts me to hear you. But we may think wrong to ourselves and others, and there's only one way we can ever hope to win peace of mind, and that is to part now and forever.

Jeam. Yes, that is all we can do now. It is cowardly to sob, and weep like a child when the road lies before me, dreary though it be. I'll leave the country, and you can think of me as though I had been drowned, and had never come back to disturb your peace of mind with memories of days that were pleasant to us.

Jean. It must be. All that I am suffering now, all the weary pain that is tugging at my heart strings at the thought of parting from you, tells me the stronger that we must meet on this earth no more. Oh, I loved you, Jeamie, very dearly—I love you yet—Lord forgive me. But I am Robin Gray's wife, and I must be faithful to him who has been good and true to me. Help me Jeamie, and go away.

Jeam. God keep you, Jeannie. I see now that I have not the worst to bear. With God's will, you shall never be troubled with the sight of me again. All that man can do to help you be a true wife, I'll do, for the sake of the love I bear you.

Jean. Go, now, and heaven guide you to happiness, if there is any in this world.   (*kissing him on the brow.*

Jeam. Farewell! Farewell!   (*exit, Jeannie by side door.*

Jeamie is going out of the cottage, when he runs against Nicol who is entering across bridge at back of stage.

Nicol. Great heaven! It cannot be you?

Jeam. Yes, it's me, unfortunately.

Nicol. And I have been mourning for you this twelve month—and you are not dead at all.

Jeam. I am sorry you have wasted so much useful grief for a child who is so ungrateful as to come to life again.

Nicol. Come to life again! Yes, it's just like that. How did it happen that you were saved?

Jeam. After drifting about on a mast for two days, I was picked up by a man-o'-war that carried me where I could not get back in a hurry.

Nicol. Now that ye are back I suppose ye have heard that your old sweetheart is married?

Jeam. Yes, I have seen her.

Nicol. Have you so? And what do you intend to do now?

Jeam. Go away again.

Nicol. (*eagerly*) When?

Jeam. As soon as I have performed a duty I owe you and others.

Nicol. What may that be?

Jeam. Did you lose much by the Colin's loss?

Nicol. (*uneasily*) Not so much as I might have done—she was very well insured.

Jeam. (*eyeing him*) Humph! Did Carrach lose anything by it?

Nicol. I couldn't say, exactly; he had a share of the cargo, and got his share of the insurance. On the other hand, he lost a heap o' time, and the chance of making something bringing a cargo home.

Jeam. (*thoughtfully*) That's queer.

Nicol. (*sharply*) What's queer?

Jeam. About Carrach! Where is he?

Nicol. He was at Greenock yesterday, and I'm expecting him here in a day or two. But what are ye driving at with these questions?

Jeam. At a serious matter to you, a matter that has ruined my— but never mind. I shall stay here till Carrach comes back.

Nicol. What for?

Jeam. To bring him to justice — and make him pay with his life for the misery he has brought on me and Jeannie.

Nicol. I do not quite understand you. But where are you going to bide?

Jeam. Not here — it's too near Cairnieford; besides I do not wish Carrach to see me.

Nicol. It would not be best if you wish to arrest him—for what I cannot imagine. But as to being near Cairnieford, I cannot see why you should trouble yourself about a 'woman who was ready to leap at the first offer she got, as soon as you were out of sight.

Jeam. Stop! I'll let no man speak ill of her in my presence.

Nicol. Just as you like. But as I was about to say — it will not do for you to stay at any of the inns, so you might go over to Askaig. There's nobody occupying the house, and you will not be particular about furniture for so short a time.

Jeam. I'll go at once.   (*exit, R.*

Nicol. He means to bring Carrach up for setting fire to the brig. There will be a fine ado if it gets wind — but it must not. I'll have to get him out of the country as quick as possible, and while he is in, keep him from getting friendly words with the agent or Robin. Devil take him! Why can't he mind his own business like other honest folks!   (*about to go, L.*

Enter, Robin Gray, passing Nicol, L.

Robin. Sharp weather.

Nicol. (*turning*) Ah, Cairnieford? Hold on a minute, I want to speak with you.

Robin. What do ye wish to say?

Nicol. I have news for you that I'm afraid will not be over welcome. (*linking arms with him.*

Robin. (*shaking him off*) I would be surprised it it was, coming from you. Well, out wi' it, let's know the worst, for I'm afraid o' nothing that you or any other man can bring against me.

Nicol. I did not say I had aught to say against you, but at times the best of us must bow the head to things we cannot help. What I have to say will trouble you or I'm mistaken.

Robin. Then in the de'il's name tell it, an' not stand there licking your choffs over it.

Nicol. Well, then, Jeames Falcon was not drowned as we all thought.

Robin. (*heartily*) I'm glad to hear't, for the lad's sake.

Nicol. Yes, but he has come back here, and been up to Cairnieford and seen your guidwife, and the Lord knows what will happen.

Robin. (*unsteadily*) Happen! What can happen?

Nicol. There's no saying, but it's an awkward business for you.

Robin. I canna' see that.

Nicol. Well, I hope you'll never need to see it; but you may count on my helping you in any way I can.

Robin. Thank you; I'm glad ye told me before I got home, as it will help me to prepare mysel'. But the sooner I'm there the better, now. Good night.

Nicol. (*aside*) The spark is touched to set the old fool's heart in a flame of jealousy. I must manage to have him catch Jeames Falcon and his wife together in a suspicious way, then there'll be an explosion, sure. I'll go and get Carrach to help me. (*exit,* R.

Robin. Aye, the sooner I'm home the better. Poor Jeannie, wife, I fear I hae wronged ye wi' my doubts. Jeannie's come home, but what o' that? We'll try to mak' the poor lad welcome, an' comfort him all we can. It's no' his fault, nor ours either, that things hae turned out as they have, so we'll just be content a's we are. Ah, here comes Jeannie now, and goodness, how pale she is.

Enter, Jeannie from the cottage.

Robin. Well met, guidwife, an' what are ye doing here this wild night?

Jean. I was here at Girzie's to get a fresh haddock for your supper, guidman.

Robin. I suppose there's been nobody at home inquiring for me the day.

Jean. No one.

Robin. You're no' looking so weel as you were when you went away this mornin'?

Jean. I have not been very well all day.

Robin. What has been the matter wi' ye?

Jean. Nothing particular. Do not trouble yourself about it—I'll be well again to-morrow.

Robin. Ye must get well, guidwife—(*laying his hand softly on her head*)—I couldna live if I was to lose ye.

Jean. How should you lose me? I am not like to die.

Robin. No, ye'll see me home yet, I hope an' expect, but Jeannie, lass, I am an old doitard body——

Jean. You're my guidman, and I'm not going to have him miscalled even by himself.

Robin. Aye, weel, guidwife, we'll let that fly stick to the wall. But at times I get notions o' things that might happen, but never will happen, then I like to hear ye say over an' over again, that ye are happy, an' that I do all ye like me to do to mak' ye so.

Jean. You have done all that a kind, good heart could do, to make me and mine happy, and while I live I'll try to prove to you that I'm grateful, and that I gave you all my heart as far as I have it to give.

Robin. An' you're no' sorry that ye married me?

Jean. No, Robin, I'm not sorry; if you be happy I never will be sorry.

Robin. It mak's me glad to hear ye say that. It would be the darkest day o' my life when I should hear ye say ye wished ye had never been married.

Jean. You shall never hear me say that.

Robin. Thank ye, lass. Folks say that marriage cools love, but that's no' true with us, for every day mak's ye the more precious to me.

Jean. Well, I'll away home and get your supper ready.

[*exit across bridge.*

Robin. Bless her! How cruel o' me to doubt her; yet what's the matter wi' her—she looks so woesome like. And she denied that any one had been at the house! Yonder comes her father—I'll question him and see if it be true Jeanie's home.

Enter, Adam, R.

Adam. Well met, Robin.

Robin. Well met, father-in-law. Hae ye seen the laird lately?

Adam. I just passed him on the road.

Robin. Did he speak?

Adam. Aye. He said good day, an' asked how ye were doing, an' said he was going to Askaig.

Robin. He didna' mention Jeames Falcon?

Adam. No.

Robin. (*moving* L.) Good night.

Adam. Good night. (*exit across bridge.*

Robin. Can it be possible that the whole story is a lie o' the laird's, and Jeames Falcon hasna' returned? I'll go in and see what Girzie knows about it. (*knocks and enters the cottage.*

Enter Girzie from the side door.

Girzie. Ah, is it yersel', Cairnieford? (*offering a chair.*

Robin. Thank ye, Girzie, but I just called to ask ye if it's true that Jeames Falcon has got back?

Girzie. Aye, it's true.

Robin. Have ye seen the lad?

Girzie. I saw him when he first came back.

Robin. I wonder he does not come to our house—we'd be glad to see him.

Girzie. So ye might be. It's easy for him that wins to forgive, but it's not so easy for him who loses.

Robin. True enough, Girzie; but I think if I was to hae a quiet chat wi' him, he might be persuaded to bear no ill will any way. Do ye know where he is?

Girzie. Somewhere about—I couldna' say exactly where.

Robin. Well, I'll gang and see if I can find him. (*exit over bridge.*
  the stage grows gradually dark, night coming on, and a storm rises

Girzie. The auld fish is beginning to smell the frying-pan! Well,
it's none o' my affair, an' I'll awa' to bed. I wonder where that
fool, Wattie is! (*exit at side door.*

Enter, Jeamie and Wattie, wet, R.

Jeam. You foolish fellow to cross the ford when the water is so
high! See what a state you're in.

Wattie. Wet to the skin, as ye must hae been that time ye most
got drooned. But I dinna care, I'm going to follow ye, for I want
to see the big king's ships with guns.

Jeam. You had better change your clothes, or you will catch
your death of cold, and go where the worms will eat you.

Wattie. I dinna want to gang there, yet I hae no other clothes to
put on.

Jeam. Well, come with me, and I'll give you these I have on,
since I am going to put on my other suit to go away in.

Wattie. Go awa'!

Jeam. Yes, since I promised Jeannie I would.

Wattie. An' tak' me too?

Jeam. Well, come along. (*they go into cottage and exit 2d. E.*

Enter, Carrach, R.

Car. There's the son o' a gun—py tam! Next time I was find
him in my power he was no got so easily off. The laird says he
threatens to pring me up for setting fire to the brig, but I was see if
he will do it—py tam! I sent Donald to pring Mrs. Gray here in
the laird's gig, as he was order me. What he was mean to do, I
dinna know or care, as long as he comes down with the silver. Yonder I hear the gig comin' now. I'll take shelter. (*hides behind bushes*

Enter, Donald and Jeannie with bundle, across bridge.

Jean. Where is my husband who is hurt and sent for me?

Donald. (*opening the cottage door*) Is he not in here? I do not
understand! Go in and sit down, and don't stir while I go and find
him.

Jean. Do so, for I must get to care for my poor Robin in his pain.
(*she sits down, and Donald goes out of cottage, and exit R.*

Enter, Jeamie, and Wattie with change of clothes, L. 2 E.

Jeam. There's your mother—go to her.

Jean. (*rising*) Jeamie?

Jeam. Jeannie!

Jean. You here? Tell me, where is my husband?

Jeam. Your husband, lass! How do I know?

Jean. Is he not here hurt? What, is it all a trick?

Jeam. What?

Jean. Oh, Jeamie, Jeamie! I did not think you would resort to
such means to gain your end.

Jeam. Gain my end! What do you mean?

Enter, Robin across bridge—he looks in the window.

Robin. The laird said I'd find them here together.

Jean. To try and take me from my husband.

Jean. Woman, are you crazy? (*Robin opens the door.*

Jean. Who's that? (*rushing to Robin*) Robin! Robin! I am glad you have come!

Robin. (*throwing her off*) Awa' woman! Dinna come near me, lest I fail to keep my hands still and do you some hurt.

Jean. Why would you seek to hurt me? Have you not come to take me home?

Robin. Home! I hae no home now, an' the Lord knows where ye will find one. How can there be a home where there is a false wife? O, woman, woman! the hoose is black wi' your shame, an' I'm a broken-down auld man who can never lift his head again.

Jean. My shame!

Robin. Aye, your shame. What! would ye brazen it out in spite o' the evidence o' my own eyes? My God! can one so guilty be so bold? Go hide your head in shame, and never look at me again, lest I strike you dead at my feet.

Jean. (*facing him boldly*) Do it now, if I deserve it. I have no cause for shame, and I will not hide my head though all the world was looking at me.

Robin. Ye hae no cause for shame? (*griping her arm and bending over her*) Was it not you who swore to be a true wife to me?

Jean. (*firmly*) Yes, and so I have been.

Robin. An' hae ye not hidden from me that this man had come home—that ye saw him? An' told me lies about yersel', an' hae ye not this nicht traveled through wind an' rain that ye might run awa' wi' him? Will ye dare to say there is no cause for shame?

Jean. I did not tell you I had seen him because I did not wish to vex you, but I meant to tell you of it. I came here to-night seeking you, not him.

Robin. Hae done, woman! I came only to satisfy mysel' that ye were here, an' the fause thing ye are, but not to stay an' add to your sin by wringing new fausehoods frae ye. I hae seen, an' I am satisfied. Tak' the road ye hae chosen, an' may ye know the misery ye hae given me. God forgive ye Jeannie, for it!

Jean. And God forgive you, Robin Gray, for the wrong you do me.

Robin. Peace, woman! Dinna let me hear ye blaspheme.

Jean. In His name I ask you to listen to me. Oh, Robin, I have been a true wife to you in thought and deed, though my heart was sorely tried. Day and night I have striven to make you happy, and prayed for strength to be all that a wife should be to you; and now, O, man! will you cast me off in your blind fury without hearing me, and leave me with a broken heart, because you are wild with jealousy? I wish you had never been goodman to me, or that I had been drowned coming here, rather than have heard your cruel, false words.

Robin. An' I would rather hae found ye dead an' cold in the stream than here wi' him.

Jean. 'Twas no fault of mine that I was here—will you not believe me?

Robin. No, after what I hae seen I am done wi' ye forever..

(*throwing her off and going.*

Jean. (*stopping him*) But you are not done with me, Cairnieford.

Robin. Out of the way, Jeames Falcon, or I canna answer for what may happen.

Jeam. I can, however.

Robin. Stand awa' frae the door, or your blood will be on my hands. I leave the woman to ye—tak' her. She's worthy o' such an honest gentleman.

Jeam. You are a mad fool. By heaven, I would give my life if she would let me take her at your word, and prove to her——

Robin. Daum ye, if ye will have it, blame yersel'.

(knocks him down and kneels on him.

Enter, Girzie, running, L.

Girzie. Lord help us! *(pulling Robin off.*

Jean. *(before Jeamie)* Robin, would you?

Robin. Keep him awa' or I'll be the death o' him! *(about to go.*

Jean. *(holding on to Robin)* I will go with you—in storm or shine I will go with you.

Robin. *(loosening her hold)* Awa'! Ye hae saved him, go to him.

Jean. And I have saved you from the gallows may be.

Robin. Awa'! Keep him out o' my sight! Ye hae saved him—ye hae ruined me. Heaven keep ye—oh, deevil burn ye forever!

(goes out of the cottage, and exit, L.

Jeam. *(about to follow)* Stop, you coward!

Girzie. *(stopping him)* Let him gang, or there'll be murder atween ye.

Jeam. Let go, I tell you.

Jean. Oh, Robin! Robin! *(falls at the door in a faint.*

Jeam. *(lifting her)* Oh, the crazy, blind idiot! Let him go, and may the black heart of him who could think the thought he has spoken of her, make a hell to him. I, for one, will never attempt to give him peace, by showing him how pure she is. Get me some water.

Wattie. I'll bring ye some. *(does so.*

Jeam. *(putting the cup to her lips)* Are you better now, Jeannie?

Jean. *(rising)* Where's Robin?

Jeam. Do not distress yourself for a man who could cast you off so lightly.

Jean. *(to Girzie)* Where is he?

Girzie. Cairnieford? He went awa' two or three minutes ago when ye fell.

Jean. *(about to go)* I will go too.

Girzie. *(interfering)* Mercy on us! Where are ye goin'?

Jean. After my husband.

Girzie. In this storm, wi' the night as dark as Egypt, an' the rain pourin'?

Jean. I must, or you must bring him back to me. I'll not stay here without him.

Girzie. Bring him back! Impossible!

Jean. Let me go away. He was angry, and may be he will be drowned.

Girzie. Deed, I hope not. If ye'll be quiet, I'll gang an' look 'round for him. Will ye bide till I come back? *(going to door.*

Jean. *(following)* No, I'll go with you.

Jeam. *(coming forward)* You shall not quit this house till morning if I have strength to keep you here. You shall not risk your life to follow a mad fool like him.

Jean. You are speaking of my husband, and if you have half the respect for me you pretend to have, you will not speak ill of him behind his back in my presence.

Jeam. I'll not speak of him at all, if you will try to calm yourself and remain. I'll show you that the respect I bear you is no pretense, for scorn him as I do, I'll go myself and seek him.

Girzie. Ye must not do that. I am acquainted wi' the bearings o' the place, an' if he'll come at all, he'll come for me. So I'll go an' gie a search. *(goes out and exit L.*

Jean. *(about to follow)* No, do not go—or let me go with you.

Jeam. *(holding her back)* Woman, bide you here.

Jean. Why are you holding me here, when my husband's life may be hangs in a balance? Have you not wrought me enough ill in bringing me here to make a good, kind man scorn me? Would you force me to remain in the same house all night with you, that there might be no chance left me of clearing myself of the shame you have brought on me?

Jeam. I had no hand in bringing you here, Jeannie — I swear it before Heaven. What gain would it be to me to shame you?

Jean. I see it now. You thought to shame me so that I would be glad to go away with you to hide myself from the scorn of the world.

Jeam. Do not speak any more. I am as blameless of the wicked thoughts as the babe unborn.

Jean. Then why did you stay here a single hour after you promised me you would go away—that we should not meet again?

Jeam. I came here to bring Wattie home.

Jean. But why did you not go away at once?

Jeam. Because I had an act of justice to you, to myself, and others to perform. I waited for Ivan Carrach to arrive. I blame him for all the misfortune that has befallen us, and was determined he should never wrong another, but that for the ruin he had wrought me, he should swing upon the gallows.

Jean. You were wrong to stay for anything.

Jeam. I know that now, but I will give up all hope of justice, and go away. You were just now afraid to remain because I would be with you—that fear need not trouble you any longer, I will go.
(turns aside, weeping.

Jean. O, woe is me! O, woe is me! *(weeping.*

Jeam. *(wiping his eyes)* Pshaw! I'm like a child. Enough, you shall never have a chance to blame me for lingering, storm or no storm. I leave you now, and so help me heaven, you shall never look on me in life again unless you beg me yourself to come to you.

Jean. I have tried you sorely, Jeamie, but I was distracted, and did not know what I was saying. Will you forgive me those words I spoke just now?

Jeam. Yes, freely.

Jean. I was wrong to blame you, wrong to fear anything that false tongues might say against us—I have no fear of them now. Stay here, then, till daylight.

Jeam. No, Jeannie. Do not try to persuade me, for I cannot yield. I am going now, perhaps to my death—shake hands, there can be no harm in that. *(offering hand.*

Jeam. *(taking it)* I think it is you who are unreasonable now. *(holding his hand)* Lord pity and help me. Why is all put upon me? Do not make me answerable for two lives.

Jean. The Lord will pity you, and help you, and if I go away now, that will be the best proof to Robin Gray of how much he has wronged us both.

Jean. (*still holding his hand*) Do not go till morning. It will be safe then. Do you not hear how the storm is raging?

Jean. Yet you would have gone out into it a few minutes ago.

Jean. But that was myself that would have been in danger, not you.

Jean. The greater the danger, the stronger is the proof that I love you more than myself—too much to give the tongue of scandal the chance of stinging you with its venom. (*kissing her hand*) Good bye, my poor lass—take courage, for the truth will come uppermost in spite of everything. Before morning I'll be miles away from here, if I am living. (*exit out of cottage, and off L.*

Wattie. (*starting up*) Hey! Jeamie Falcon! Bide a minute till I get my hat, and I'll go wi' ye. (*gets hat and follows across bridge.*

Jean. He was right—for his own sake and mine, to go away at once in spite of tempest and darkness. And why should I stay here? There's nobody to hinder me now, and it is right I should go to my home though I die on the way. Lord forgive me the thought, but I feel that I would rather die and get away from this weary sorrow that is hard, hard to bear.

She opens the door and looks out. By this time Wattie, after groping about, reaches the bridge, and Carrach coming up behind him, grasps him—they then wrestle, and just as there is a flash of lightning, Crrrach throws Wattie over the crag, he giving a yell, and Jeannie witnessing the deed in the flash. Tableau and

END OF ACT THIRD.

ACT IV.

SCENE FIRST.—Public parlor in the Port Inn. Main door at back in C., with window R., door and window L., door R. Table, chairs and other furniture about the room. Sandy, David, and others discovered talking.

Sandy. I doubt not but that there's been a fine squabble between them.

David. Between who?

San. Between the mistress and her goodman. Cairnieford went off last night after her in such a fury as I never saw him in before—and did you not notice the face of the mistress?

Dav. Yes, she looked scared like.

San. Take my word for it, there's been a fine squabble, and I don't think we've got to the end of it yet.

Dav. I can't surmise what they would quarrel about—can you!

San. The word has been out since yesterday that Jeames Falcon had come home, and was hanging around clean crazy at finding Jeannie married to Cairnieford.

Dav. It's true enough that Jeamie come home, for I saw him myself and spoke to him, but he was so ugly like, I did not stop to talk. Yonder Mrs. Gray comes back—let's go back. (*all exit, L.*

Enter, Adam, Jeannie and Girzie, R.

Jean. Well, father, what did you find out?

Adam. Nothing whatever is known at Clashgirn o' Jeames Falcon, or his whereabout.

Girzie. What'll I do to find Wattie?

Jean. You'll have to find Jeamie. He's the only one that can tell you where Wattie is, and no doubt they are together.

Girzie. Find him! Aye, though I should travel from land's end to land's end I must find him. But he could na' be so thoughtless as to let him go wi' him. He's may be sent him home afore now. I must haste after him, wherever he is. (*exit, C.*

Adam. Where's Monduff?

Jean. Gone to bring Robin. What I was going to tell you, father, I'll tell you now in his presence, and I look to you to make him hear me.

Adam. No fear o' that—he's no' an unreasonable man.

Jean. You do not know the state he's in, father, or what he is thinking.

Adam. No, I canna' mak' out what the quarrel is about, an' it clean bamboozles me.

Jean. He thinks—(*with faltering voice*)—he thinks I was going to run away with Jeamie Falcon.

Adam. What would ye do that for? Ye never would disgrace them who had been true an' kind to ye, even in your thought.

Jean. Never, father, never.

Adam. I couldna' think ye would, Jeannie, an' I wonder that Robin could so far forget himsel' as to doubt ye. But what was the cause o' it?

Jean. You shall hear it all in his presence. Yonder they come, I'll stand aside for a while. (*stands aside*

Enter Robin and Monduff, at C.

Robin. I didna' expect to come here, Adam, but Monduff said ye would speak wi' me, an' may be it is as well I have come.

Monduff. I scarcely expected to bring ye here an hour ago. Man, you gave us all a scare.

Adam. How was that?

Mon. His horse was found dead in the stream, an' we thought to find him in the same place.

Robin. Poor brute! I might ha' been wi' him. But sit down, —(*they sit. To Adam*)—Ye wanted to speak wi' me?

Adam. Aye. Ye had a quarrel wi' your guidwife I hear. I thought ye was a man o' too much sense to mak' an ado like this.

Robin. I'm glad ye thought that, Adam, because ye'll be readier to believe that I'm no' like to mak' such a stir without good reason for it.

Adam. When I know your reason, I'll be the better able to gie ye my opinion.

Robin. I see that ye think me in the wrong. Would to heaven that I had been so, but there's no use wishing for harvest in December.

Adam. Well.

Robin. What I wanted to tell ye Adam, was that I'm goin' awa' the morn. I dinna where to, or when I'll come back, maybe never. While I'm awa' I want you to take care o' the farm an' keep things in order, so that if she should ever come back, she may find a home an' friends ready to receive her.

Adam. Who is it ye're talking about?

Robin. My wi—your daughter.

Adam. What about her coming home? She's come home.

Robin. Come home! When?

Adam. As soon as ever she could get across the stream. What else would she do, or where else would she go?

Robin. Oh, aye! I understand! She's been frightened by what I said last night, and has come home instead o' goin' wi' him. But that doesna' mak' her the less guilty.

Adam. Guilty o' what?

Robin. Guilty o' deceivin' me—guilty o' deceivin' the man she had sworn to abide by till death, by goin' awa' wi' Jeames Falcon.

Adam. Ye are speakin' o' my daughter, sir, an' ye are speakin' *lies.* Jeannie Lindsay was never guilty o' the shame ye charge her wi', even in her thoughts.

Robin. Are ye sure o' that? Then will ye tell me why she hid from me that she had seen Falcon; hid it from ye, too, unless ye're more a hypocrite than I thought. Will ye tell me what for Falcon should lurk an' keep out o' the way o' me who's aye been his friend? Will ye tell me why she met him at Brownie's Bite where I saw them together wi' my own eyes?

Adam. (*brings Jeannie forward*) Here's my daughter—she'll answer for hersel'.

Robin. (*going*) Let me go, then.

Mon. (*detaining him*) Hoots, man! Be sensible and hear what she has to say.

Robin. I told her never to come near me again, but that there may be no blame on me, I'll listen to what she has to say.

Jean. You blame me because I did not tell you I had seen Jeannie. I did not do so because I wished to wait until I could speak of him without giving you the pain of thinking I cared more for him than a wife should.

Robin. Ye hear that? She owns herself that she could not speak o' him as the wife of another man should.

Jean. You knew when I married you, that I loved him, and that I would never have been your wife if I had not believed him dead. I did not mean to remind you of this, but you have forced it from me.

Robin. Say what you will—I can bear it.

Jean. If you had said a word about him, I would have told you everything, but you did not although you knew he was at home. I did not speak, for that day him and me parted never to meet again in this world as we thought.

Robin. An' no doubt ye had no expectations o' seeing him at Brownie's Bite when ye went there last night, taking your clothes wi' ye, as if ye didna' mean to come home again.

Jean. I did not think of him at all. A man came to the house and said you was hurt, having had a quarrel with Jeames Falcon, and for me to go at once and bring some clothes lest I should not be able to get home that night. I went with him in a gig, never doubting his word, my mind so much taken up with you.

Robin. Who was the man?

Jean. I did not know him.

Robin. Humph! An' do ye think a man in his senses is to believe that story?

Jean. You would believe me if you were in your senses, Robin Gray; but you are possessed by some evil spirit that makes everything you hear sound false as your own suspicions are. Lord help you, man—I almost forget my own pain and pity you.

Robin. Thank ye. Was that all ye had to tell us?

Jean. No. When we got to Brownie's Bite, nobody was in the house. I was surprised, and the man said he could not understand it, but if I would sit down he would go and find you. He went, but did not return. But this I noticed—the gig was Clashgirn's, and no doubt the laird can tell you who the man was who had his gig.

Robin. Oh, I can tell without his help—it was just a man sent by Jeames Falcon.

Jean. I will not believe it. He would not be guilty of so base a trick on me. I blamed him for it when I was driven wild by your abuse, but I am sorry for it now.

Robin. Humph! Are ye?

Adam. Go on, Jeannie.

Jean. I waited about five minutes, when Jeamie Falcon came in with Wattie Todd. He was as much put out at sight of me as I was of him. Then you came, and know what happened after, except that Jeamie went away just after yourself, saying that we would never see him again—(*eyeing Robin*

Adam. What?

Jean. Something that frightened me, and I swooned and fell. I did not come to myself till this morning, when as soon as I could, I came home. That is all I have to tell.

Adam. An' every word ye have spoken I believe to be true in the sight o' heaven.

Robin. And I believe it to be as false as hell.

Adam. What. (*lifting his hand to strike him*)

Jean. (*preventing him*) Father! Father!

Adam. Ye're not the man I took ye to be, and it's a doom's black day for me that I must feel mysel' beholding as I am to the man who could speak as ye have done o' my daughter. By the Lord, if I had the use o' my arm as once I had, I would have broken every bone in your body for half as much.

Jean. Hush, father. Don't speak so—it can do no good, and you have more need to pity than be angry with him, for he'll see the day he'll rue what he has said—God pity him.

Mon. I never like to meddle between man and wife, but Carnieford I must say I think ye are wrong.

Robin. God forgive me, woman, if I have wronged ye. Oh, Jeannie, I would be proud to have the tongue that has spoken your shame burnt out o' my mouth if I could only feel that ye have spoken the truth.

Jean. What have I ever done that you can only believe I am telling lies?

Robin. Ye hid from me that he had come back, an' ye have told me — though yesterday ye said ye would never — that ye wished ye had never been my wife?

Jean. And you drove me to it with your cruel words. You have said enough this day to almost make me wish I had gone away with Jeanie Falcon last night.

Robin. Ye hear her Monduff? Ye hear her Adam?

Jean. (*with a proud look*) I did not mean to say any more to you. A man who is ready to snap at any word that could cast shame on his wife, is not the one to do her justice,

Robin. I have tried to do my duty by ye——

Jean. And I have never failed in mine. But it ends all here—the last word I will ever speak to defend myself is spoken.

Robin. As ye think best. I'll arrange with Carnegie the lawyer, so that the woman who bears my name shall never want.

Jean. I will have nothing from you as long as I can work for myself. We need not stay here any longer, father—all has been said that need be.

Adam. There's just a word, and that is, to tell you Cairnieford that my arm is nearly well, an' wi' heaven's help I'll work night an' day to pay ye back every penny we owe ye.

Mon. Hoot! Toot! This is not the way to part. Come, Cairnieford, just say ye have been wrong, an' you goodwife, just give him your hand.

Jean. No, I can never give my hand again till I have proof that his mind is as free from doubt as the day we were married.

Adam. She shall never gie him her hand again wi' my will, though he should get down on his knees an' beg her to forgie him.

Jean. I cannot go away without telling you that I never knew how much I cared for you till now, when we are parting, may be never to see each other, or speak a kind word again. But it must be so; for your sake and mine, too, we will be better apart.

- (*exit with Adam, c. d.*)

Mon. Well, it beats all, that two folks as fond of each other as can be, will make their lives miserable, just because one of them has not the courage to say 'forget and forgive.' I'll call her back.

Robin. No, it will do no good—better let her go.

Mon. But this will never do—you must come to a right understanding.

Robin. I see no way o' bringing it about.

Mon. Well, you come home with me to-night, an' after you have had a good sleep your head will be clearer, and may be you'll be able to see then.

Robin. Very weel; I'll follow ye soon, but I'm going to speak to Clashgirn first, who I see is comin'. (*exit Monduff, c. d.*) If this be one o' Nicol McWhapple's tricks to fool me, by the Lord above, it'll be the dearest bit o' knavery he ever played.

Enter, Nicol McWhapple with bottle and glasses, r.

Nicol. (*sitting at table*) Hallo! Is that you, Cairnieford? Come and have a dram. (*pouring out a glass*

Robin. No, thank ye. I'm sorry to disturb ye, but ye have it in your power to serve me.

Nicol. In what way, Cairnieford?

Robin. By answering a few questions. When did you leave Jeames Falcon last?

Nicol. Od! It's extraordinar! Every body must think I keep him tied to my coat tail, for it's always to me they come asking after him.

Robin. When did ye see him last, I was asking?

Nicol. (*studying*)· Oom! Let me see! Hoot! yes, I mind — it was on yesterday afternoon.

Robin. Then it was you who sent the gig to Cairnieford last night to take my guidwife to Brownie's Bite?

Nicol. In the name of goodness, what should I do that for?

Robin. Ye need na' try to hide it from me. An' it was ye who sent for her wi' the lieing message that me an' Falcon had been quarreling, an' that I had got hurt. Curse ye, if ye don't confess the whole truth before I leave this room, ye'll sup sorrow wi' a big spoon ere I'm done wi' ye.   ,   (*threatening him*

Nicol. I didn't intend to say a word, but since ye put me to it in self defense, it is necessary that I should speak.

Robin. Out wi' it, then.

Nicol. I'll begin by telling you that I have heard all that happened at Brownie's Bite yestere'en from Girzie Todd, and my opinion is that Jeames Falcon, who is do doubt making his way out of the country, is a young villain. As for your wife——

Robin. Weel, what about her?

Nicol. I'll not say what about her.

Robin. (*clutching him by the throat*) Say an ill word o' her an' I'll throttle ye, by heaven.

Nicol. I wouldn't stand this treatment, only I know in what distress of mind you are in, and pity you.

Robin. Go on, will ye! Curse ye!

Nicol. Well, Jeames Falcon got the loan of the gig last night, for what purpose I did not know, or he'd never had it. My opinion now is, that whether your goodwife was a party to the arrangement or not—and I'll not pretend to say—he was meaning to take her away with him, when you came upon them and frightened one or both of them, so they did not carry out their intention.

Robin. That is all I wish to know. Good day.   (*exit*, C. D.

Nicol. Curse it and burn it.   (*raising the glass*

Enter, Carrach, R.

Carrach. (*snatching the glass*) Oich, no! She would shust as soon trink it.

Nicol. You again! What do you want now?

Car. She'll look in, and she was see there was nopody but yer-sel', and she was be dry.

Nicol. Well, drink then, I'll not stint you, for it's my opinion you'll not drink many more glasses unless old Nick deals in his own liquor.

Car. What'll you do then?

Nicol. Me? Nothing.

Car. What'll you give if I was go?

Nicol. There's no use saying what I might do, seeing you are bound to stay unless I do what I cannot.

Car. Say your spoke, and then we'll know.

Nicol. Well, I'll give you the schooner, since you have taken such a notion for her, and a hundred pounds beside, if you'll sign this paper and go away.   (*showing a paper*

Car. The hundred in gold?

Nicol. If you like.

Car. (*looking at the paper*) What's in the paper?

Nicol. Just an acknowledgement of two or three things that would give me the power to hand you over to the sheriff's officers should you ever set foot in this land again.

Car. When'll she get the money?

Nicol. The day after to-morrow.

Car. Very goot; pring the money and the paper to the schooner then, and I was make my cross on the paper like a man. And may she be droont in whiskey if you'll ever have a chance to use it against Ivan Carrach—pe-tam. (*exit, R.*

Enter, Monduff C. D., *followed by Sandy, David and others, bearing a body.*

Sandy. It's a bad job!

David. Aye, it's a bad job!

Mon. It is sad to think that after passing safely through the perils of fire, tempest and sea, the poor fellow should have come home to perish in this miserable manner.

Sandy. You'd better send one of the lads for fiscal Smart — he'll know what to do. (*exit David, C. D.*) Another had better go over to Clashgirn and tell the laird.

Mon. There's the laird yonder. (*pointing to him*

Nicol. (*rising*) What's that you have there?

Sandy. It's Jeamie Falcon, and oh, what a sight!

Nicol. (*staggering*) Heavens above!

Mon. (*offering his arm*) Take my arm, laird, it's a sore sight ye have to look on, but we must bow to His will.

Nicol. Thank you, Mr. Monduff, I can walk alone. (*shivering and leaning heavily on his staff*) It was the shock of the news that upset me, but you know I have never murmured at the will of Providence —I have always humbly bowed before it, and I do that now.

Sandy. Will you look at the corpse, laird? (*uncovering it*

Nicol. Hide it! Hide it away from my eyes.

(*he shrinks back and turns away*

Sandy. (*to Monduff*) I never expected him to take on that way; he never did anything to my knowledge to show that he was dreadful fond of him when living.

Mon. But he feels it more now he is dead.

Nicol. (*advancing*) It's a dreadful sight, Mr. Monduff. Ye cannot blame me if I am a little more upset than a christian man should be about any mere worldly loss, but I liked the lad well.

(*shivering and turning away*

Enter Sheriff Smart and David, C. D.

Smart. Where's the body?

Sandy. (*lifting the covering*) Here, sheriff.

Smart. (*examining it*) This is no case of accident—it is *murder!*

All. Murder!

Smart. Yes, strangulation by some one with tar on his hand.

Mon. It is not possible that any one could have lifted a hand against him, for he was liked by all who knew him.

Smart. Probably, probably! Who found the body?

Sandy. I did.

Smart. (*taking notes*) And you identified it at once?

Sandy. Yes; I knew Jeames Falcon before he went to sea, and I saw him yesterday with these clothes on. But the laird here can speak to that as well as me, for he was a friend of his.

Smart. (*to Nicol*) And you also identified it?

Nicol. I'm sorry to say that I have no doubt it is my poor friend, for I saw him with those clothes on no later than last night.

Smart. Where was he last seen alive?

Nicol. At Brownie's Bite, I believe.

Smart. Then he was not living with you?

Nicol. (*shaking his head mournfully*) No, I wished he had been.

Smart. How was that, when you liked him so well?

Nicol. He wanted to get far away from his sweetheart who got married.

Smart. Oh, his lass married! What is her name now?

Nicol. Mistress Gray.

Smart. And where does she live now?

Nicol. At Cairnieford.

Smart. Yes, yes; I remember now—a daughter of Adam Lindsay the fisher—a fine body, a fine body. (*to Nicol*) Are you a relation of the deceased?

Nicol. Yes, a kind of one.

Smart. Then, may be you would not mind sending up a cart to remove the body?

Nicol. Certainly; but can I take it to my house?

Smart. There's no reason why you should not.

Nicol. And I would like to bury him. It's the last service I can do him, who thought he would have been here to do that for me as my friend and heir.

Smart. Oh, you intended him to be your heir? Yes, you may bury him when you like after the doctor has examined him.

Nicol. Thank you; that is one small consolation at least.

(*all exit with the body, L.*)

Enter, Robin Gray and Carnegie, C. D.

Robin. Weel, here ye are at last! What kept ye?

Carnegie. An awful thing, that's given me such a shock.

Robin. Never mind telling what it was. Have ye brought a' the papers?

Carnegie. (*giving him papers*) Aye, here they all are, ready to sign.

Robin. Wrote out as I told ye, making over everything to her, an' leaving it a' in her own name to have an' to hand.

Carnegie. Yes.

Robin. (*sitting down to sign*) Weel, where'll I sign?

Carnegie. There—(*showing him*)—but who's that?

Enter, Monduff, C. D.

Oh, it's you, Monduff? I'm glad.

Mon. Thank ye, but it's Cairnieford I wish to see, Mr. Carnegie.

Carnegie. There he is, and if you can persuade him to take time and consider what he is about to do, it is more than I can do.

Robin. For heaven's sake let there be no more said about it. I tell ye there's no power on earth to mak' me change my mind. I'm going awa', an' I want to leave things so that whatever may happen to me, she may never come to want.

Mon. I am here to deliver a message, although I will not refuse any advice or assistance you may ask and I give.

Robin. Who is the message from?

Mon. Your wife. She bade me say that the body of Jeames Fal-

'con has been found in the stream, and you are to do what you think best under the circumstances.

Robin. I canna' say that I'm sorry for him as I would once hae been, for he's made my life a burden to me, and a curse. He has made me out an outcast, without friends or home. I'm no' sorry for him.

Mon. Hark! *(knocking* C. *he bolts the door*

Carnegie. What's wrong, minister?

Mon. Listen, Carnieford. I believe that's the fiscal and the sheriff's officer—have you no cause to fear them?

Robin. Me? What for should I fear them?

Mon. You are sure? There is still time for you to get out by the back window. For your wife's sake — Carnegie and I will turn our backs while you escape, if you wish to do so.

Robin. What would I be going out by the window for, when the door's there?

Mon. You remember what I told you—Falcon's body has been found.

Robin. An' what in the deil's name has that to do wi' me an' the window?

Mon. Then I may open the door?

Robin. Surely. *(Monduff opens the door*

Enter Smart and others, C.

Smart. Hallo, Cairnieford, you're here. It's a while since I have seen you; how are you getting on? I heard you were about to travel? *(grasping his hand.*

Robin. Aye, it's true.

Smart. I'm sorry to hear it. Well, before you go, will you part with that cow you bought at the Lammas fair? I'll give you ten pounds. Come, say the word—is it a bargain? *(opens Robin's hand as if to put the money in*

Robin. I canna bargain wi' ye for anything in the present state o' my affairs. *(rising*

Smart. I would rather some one else had the job in hand, but since there is no help for it I must do my duty. Robin Gray, you are my prisoner. *(seizing him*

Robin. What do ye mean? What hae I done?

Smart. You are charged with the murder of James Falcon.

Robin. It's an infernal lie, an' ye shall never mak' me a prisoner on such a charge. I hated the man, an' when I found him an' my wife together, the deevil was strong in me to fell him on the spot, but I ran awa' from the place so that I might not be tempted more than I could bear, an' I have not seen him since. I'll answer for all that I have done in any court, but ye shall no' drag me to jail like a common thief, as long as I have strength in my arms to keep ye off. *(swinging staff*

Smart. Your resistance only makes things look the worse against you.

Mon. If you are innocent, Cairnieford, go with Mr. Smart quietly. That will be the best and firmest denial of the charge which he feels compelled to make against you. Be calm, I beseech you, and not by your rashness add to the difficulties of your position. For your wife's sake as well as your own, be careful what you do.

Robin. Aye, there's the thing o't. To think that this all comes o'

caring too much about her. Well, well, what needs I care for life
or anything that may befall me? The worst an' the best of it is, we
can only die once. (*throwing away staff*) I'll go wi' ye, fiscal,
peacefully. Do ye want to put me in irons? (*holding out hands*)
Here, put your hand-cuffs on my wrists and your shackles on my
feet—do wi' me as ye like—I dinna mind anything now.

Smart. There will be no necessity for such desperate precautions.
You'll only have to come over to the jail with me, and you'll have
to let a turnkey sleep in the same cell—I mean room with you—
that's all, and I give you my word that you shall be treated with the
respect due to a man who may be able to prove himself innocent.

Robin. Thank ye.

Mon. And until you have failed to do that, do not think that
your friends will forsake you.

Robin. Friends? I hae a few o' them, but if I had thousands
they could never gie me back the peace I hae lost, or clear the guid
name that's trampled in the mire this night.

Enter Adam and Jeannie, C. D.

Jean. (*running to him*) Robin, my husband! my husband!

Robin. (*throwing her off*) Off, woman! Is it not enough that
ye hae brought me to this disgrace, but ye maun come to affront me
in my humiliated state, and add insult to injury!

Jean. (*sinking on her knees*) O, woe is me! O, woe is me!

TABLEAU—CURTAIN.

ACT V.

*SCENE FIRST.—Sheriff's department in the jail. Heavy barred
door to the back, door and window L., two doors R. Table with writing
material and chairs in the room. The Sheriff and Jeannie discovered.*

Smart. (*writing at the table*) Well, Mrs. Gray, I am a friend of
your husband; let that be distinctly understood between us, and
you'll easily see that the questions I am going to ask you are as
much for his own benefit, as because they come in the way of my
duty.

Jean. I'm glad you are his friend, sir, and I'll try and answer
your questions.

Smart. Sit down then, and make yourself as comfortable as you
can.   (*writing her answer down*)

Jean. Thank you.   (*sitting down*)

Smart. You were at Brownie's Bite on Tuesday night last?

Jean. I was.

Smart. What took you there?

Jean. A man came after me with a gig, and took me there to at-
tend my husband, who had got hurt, so he said.

Smart. And while you were there Cairnieford arrived and had
some words with you and James Falcon?

Jean. (*with difficulty*) Yes.

Smart. Well, after you had separated, what then?

Jean. I was left alone in the house.

Smart. Did you look out of the house after them?

Jean. I did.

Smart. Did you see anything?

Jean. It was very dark.

Smart. Yes, but there was lightning, you might have seen something when it flashed.

Jean. It was raining very hard, and the lightning dazzled my eyes.

Smart. Well, you heard something at any rate?

Jean. (*with emotion*) Oh, man, how can you expect me to be willing to answer what may be the death of my husband?

Smart. Then you did hear a cry?

Jean. Yes, heaven help me, I did.

Smart. And after that you fainted?

Jean. Oh, ask me no more about it.

Smart. Come, Mrs. Gray, I'm sorry to trouble you, but I have a little more to ask you. What was it frightened you into the faint?

Jean. (*chokingly*) I cannot rightly say what.

Smart. Was it your husband's voice?

Jean. I could not say. I did not see him.

Smart. But you heard him, and that was what frightened you, and you fainted.

Jean. Who told you that? Robin?

Smart. That's neither here nor there. But you have seen him since then—I mean since you got home from Brownie's Bite?

Jean. Yes, I saw him on Wednesday.

Smart. And did you know he was going to leave the country?

Jean. He said he was going away.

Smart. What was his reason for that?

Jean. Nothing but the quarrel between him and me—and that has been the cause of all his trouble and mine. Oh, sir, do not ask any more questions, I have nothing more to tell you, and you are rending my heart with every word.

Smart. I'll relieve you in a minute, Mrs. Gray. (*handing paper*) If you'll read this over and sign it, if there's nothing in it you object to.

Jean. (*looking at it*) Must I sign it?

Smart. I am afraid I will have to insist, unless there is something in it you think you have not said.

Jean. There is nothing—but—

Smart. You are afraid it will go against him? But you must not lose heart; I hope he'll come through all right.

Jean. (*signing it*) Do you think that? Oh, sir, do you think that?

Smart. I hope so, Mrs. Gray. I must try to find the man who brought the gig for you, as he might give the affair a new turn.

Jean. Then I'll find him!

Smart. How do you propose to seek him?

Jean. I do not know yet, but will you let me see my good man for a minute. I have just one word to speak to him. Oh, sir, do not refuse, he is in sore need of some one to bid him keep up his heart, and may be if he knows that I'm trying to save him it will give him courage to bear the cruel shame that's on him.

Smart. Yes, you can see him, and I wish you may be able to cheer him, for he's more downcast than any man I ever saw. Wait a while. (*exit, Smart.* R.

Jean. God strengthen and sustain me in t..is, my hour of trial.

Enter Turnkey, R., *who opens the* C. *door, and then stands apart.*
Enter Robin, C. D.

. *Robin.* Jeannie!   *(turning away*

Jean. I see you are not pleased that I should come near you, even when in such sore need of friends as you are now, but I will not trouble you long.

Robin. I wasna' expecting ye.

Jean. No. You thought that I would leave you to whatever might happen, without trying to help you, but I could not. I do not care what you may think of me, but I could not sit idle at home and know you needed help without trying to give it to you.

Robin. I'm thankfu' to ye.

Jean. I did not seek your thanks, I did not need them. With heaven's will I shall do what a wife should do for you in your trouble.

Robin. I'm thankfu' to ye.

Jean. I have just one question to ask, and after that I'll not trouble you any more with my presence.

Robin. I'm listening.

Jean. Did you meet Jeames Falcon after you left me in Girzie's house? Did you see him again, or hear him again, or come near him in any way?

Robin. Ye, too, doubt me. But what else could I expect. Ye, who never cared for me and loved him; what could ye be but the first one to think me guilty?

Jean. Oh, man! do not speak those cruel false words now—but answer me—answer me from your heart, truly, as though you were at the judgement seat, and give me strength to save you.

Robin. I never saw him, or heard him, or came near him, to my knowledge, after I left him and you in Girzie's house.

Jean. God be thanked—God be thanked for that—I believe you—though you did not believe me when I told you the truth.

Robin. Woman! Woman! I am cast down wi' shame.

Jean. Do not be downcast, you shall not die the death of shame. Heaven will not let it be; and there is one who will never rest, day or night, till all that looks black against you is made clear.

Robin. Jeannie, Jeannie, ye mak' my heart ache wi' the thought o' the wrong I hae done ye. Oh, I hae been mad—mad, and God help me, I only see it now when maybe it is too late—Jeannie!

(holding out his arms towards her, she is about to rush to him when

Smart enters R.

Smart. Excuse me for interrupting you, Mr. and Mrs. Gray, but two smuggler prisoners have arrived, whom I wish to question here. Will you please retire with your husband into his own cell—I should say room—where you can continue your interview undisturbed.

Jean. Certainly.

He sees them into the back room, then motions the Turnkey to bring in the prisoner.

Smart. Bring in Carrach first. *(sitting at table—exit turnkey,* L., *and re-enter with Carrach in irons)* Well, man, you are here, arrested on a certain charge. What have you to say for yourself?

Car. No' caring what the charge 'll be, she'll no' h   .hing
to say.

Smart. The evidence is strong against you, so you had better give
a full confession of the facts, and maybe clear yourself.

Car. Was that sae? Oich, but she was sorry for it. And who's
was the evidence—no' the lairds?

Smart. (*aside*) Ah! so the laird is implicated? Yes, and Donald, your mate's.

Car. Did they told you all apout it?

Smart. Yes.

Car. Then what 'll you want me to told you again for?

Smart. For your own sake, and to get at the truth as near as
possible.

Car. Heh—and whar's the laird?

Smart. He'll soon not be far off from you.

Car. Whar was that?

Smart. In the next cell to yours, a prisoner like yourself. (*aside*)
Surely that will make him speak out.

Car. The laird in shail? That was a fall doon. Weel, you'll
shust go to him, he'll told you what you'll want to know. I'll
no' spoke a word—py tam.

Smart. Then you'll not answer any questions?

Car. No, it was dry work to spoke when she'll have no whiskey,
and she'll no' spoke a say.

Smart. (*to Turnkey*) Take this stubborn brute off and bring in
the mate. (*exit, Turnkey with Carrach*) The prospects are these
men have been engaged with the laird in more deviltry than smuggling.

Re-enter Turnkey with Donald, in irons, 2 E. L.

Donald. What am I brought here for, I'd like to know? I have
done nothing wrong, and by— (*aside—seeing Smart*) The Fiscal!

Smart. (*looking up*) We have not been the best of friends, still I
wish to help you out of this scrape, if you say you are innocent and
are sensible enough to tell the truth.

Don. I have done nothing to bring me into the scrape. I know
nothing to tell.

Smart. Well, you will be likely to keep Carrach company in the
cell, perhaps on the gal— (*knocking heard*) Open that door!
(*the Turnkey opens the back door, and*

Jeannie enters suddenly.

Jean. (*pointing to Donald*) That's the man!

Smart. What man?

Jean. The man who brought me in the gig to Brownie's Bite, and
told me the lie that my husband was hurt.

Don. I did no more than obey Carrach's orders, and if harm came
out of it, it was not my fault.

Smart. (*aside*) Ho, ho! This is the rascality they think they
have been arrested for, and in which the laird is implicated! You
had better make a clean breast of it; holding your tongue will not
help Carrach, and will do yourself harm.

Don. What is it you want to know?

Smart. All about how and why you came to take Mrs. Gray to
Brownie's Bite.

Don. Well, the skipper gave me orders, and I went to the laird's after the gig, and took it down to Cairnieford for you, and said what I was told to say, then took you where I was told to take you, as you know.

Jean. Was this Carrach the skipper of the Colin?

Don. Yes. He sailed it for the laird.

Jean. What? Oh, I see it all now, thank God! I see it all!

Smart. See it all! What? Explain yourself.

Jean. Send him off.

Smart. Take him back to his cell. (*exit Turnkey and Donald*) Well, Mrs. Gray.

Jean. Jeames Falcon told me himself, that awful night, that the reason why he staid in Portlappoch was to bring this Carrach to justice for some ill he had done him.

Smart. What ill?

Jean. The ill was the burning of the Colin, which has been the cause of all his misfortune.

Smart. Yes; but Mrs. Gray, what has the laird to do with all this.

Jean. The laird, as owner of the vessel, probably knew of its being set on fire, but did not object, as he had a heavy insurance on it, and wishing to get James out of the way, they together planned the affair at Brownie's Bite. Ah, Robin, the worst is past now, you will yet be free.

Smart. I hope the worst is past, Mrs. Gray, but your husband will not be safe until we can prove some one else committed the murder.

Jean. We know now what will force the laird to speak.

Smart. He'll say nothing as long as he can avoid it. I'll go now and get out a warrant for his arrest, anyway. I'll meet you here in an hour.

(*exit, L.*

Enter Carnegie and Hutcheson, R.

Carn. Ah, Mrs. Gray, you are here! I have been seeking you. Here to see your good man, I suppose?

Jean. Yes, and I have now got what will force the laird to give me the proof of Robin's innocence.

Carn. What have you?

Jean. Carrach and his mate, the man who brought in the gig, are both here in the jail, and the man has confessed enough to force Clashgirn to clear Robin of the murder of Jeames Falcon.

Carn. We have the proof already, if what this man says is true.

Jean. What does he say?

Carn. He says that James Falcon has cheated us a second time, and he's not dead at all!

Jean. My God! Can it be possible?

Carn. So this man says.

Jean. Whose corpse is it then that was found?

Carn. I'm fairly at my wit's end to know. Everybody said it was Falcon's.

Jean. Did you see the body?

Carn. No.

Jean. Then I'll go and look at it, and I will force the laird to explain what looks so dark.

Carn. I wish you would. I'll be ready to go with you directly; I have just to settle one or two things about Carrach first.

Jean. You will not set him free?

Carn. No; although we cannot charge him with the murder, we can keep him on another charge. Hutcheson declares that the signature to the statement of the crew, about the burning of the Colin, was not his, and is consequently a forgery. Aha! We'll bind him tight enough on that.   *(sitting down to write*

Jean. (to Hutcheson) Where is Jeamie Falcon, and why does he not come here?

Hutch. He'll not here, mistress. I left him aboard the vessel out in the bay; he bade me come ashore to see Mr. Carnegie about the Colin business, and said if he wanted to see him he must come where he was, for he had promised never to set foot in this place again.

Jean. Can you go and see him now?

Hutch. I do not know, but I can try.

Jean. See him then, and tell him that it was me that begged and prayed him for the sake of all that's past and gone, between him and me, to come back and save my husband's life, who lies in jail on his account.

Hutch. I'll do your will.

Jean. Bring him here to Mr. Smart. If its true that he's living still, he will come when you say that it was me who sent for him.

Carn. Sign this, Hutcheson. *(he signs paper)* Now seek Falcon and bring him here as soon as possible. That's the first thing, and the first thing you have got to do, Mrs. Gray, is to learn who it is that has been murdered, and how the mistake was made in his identity.   *(exit, Hutcheson, R.*

Jean. I see it all now, sir. I see it all.

Carn. How—what?

Jean. The body that was found the folk all said was Jeamie Falcon's, so there must have been something about it to make them think so.

Carn. Yes, what then?

Jean. It was the clothes. Now Carrach went by stealth to kill James Falcon, and in the dark mistook Wattie Todd, who somehow had his suit on for him.

Carn. That may be, but say nothing about it at present. The argument acts both ways, and may be used against Cairnieford as well as for him. Who is that coming?

Enter Hutcheson, R.

Carn. You are soon back?

Jean. Have you seen him?

Hutch. I got word to him sooner than I expected, and that's how I'm so soon back.

Jean. (eagerly) Have you seen him?

Hutch. Yes, mistress, and I'm looking for him here every minute.

Jean. Are you sure he will come?

Hutch. Why, should he not come? The minute I acquainted him that it was you who had sent for him, he bade me come here and tell you to wait for him.

Enter Jeamie, R.

Jean. O, thank God!

Jeam. You sent for me, and I have come, Mrs. Gray, as I said I would only when you yourself prayed for me to come to you.

Jean. I sent for you to ask you to help me save my husband from a death of shame.

Jeam. (turning his head away) Me?

Jean. You will not refuse to satisfy Robin how much he has wronged both you and me in his thoughts, by proving yourself his best friend in the hour of his sore need?

Jeam. (*covering his face*) I, his friend?

Jean. For my sake. Jeannie; for the sake of all I have borne on your account, and you on mine, save him. Do not refuse me this.

Jeam. Me save him? That's a hard job you ask me to undertake —harder than you seem to think. But all your pity is for him, you have none for me, although I have lost and he has won what I lost. It is against nature for me to try to restore him to the happiness that his life bars me from forever—the happiness I think him unworthy of after the scorn he has cast on you.

Jean. Hush, Jeamie! Do not speak that way, he was deceived by false tongues, and blinded with passion. I would not ask you to do this, but that there is nobody who can help him as you can, if you will.

Jeam. I did not come to speak that way; I came to learn what you sought of me, and to do your bidding. You have asked more than I thought I could do, even for you, and that made me forget myself. But it's the last time you shall ever hear from me about what's past and gone. The lassie who filled life with hope and light to me is dead, but for her sake, for the sake of the sweet memory she has left me, I will do what I can for you, even to helping Robin Gray.

Jean. Thank you, Mr. Falcon.

Carn. The first thing we want to know then, Jeames, is whose body is this that has been taken for yours?

Jeam. Wattie Todds, with my clothes on.

Carn. Just that. Well now, we want to know how he came to have your clothes on, that you were seen wearing that very afternoon?

Jeam. The poor lad took it into his head to follow me, to see the big ships with guns, as he said, and crossing the ford after me he got wet to the skin. So I forced him to put on a cast off suit of mine, and it was just then we went into the house and found Mrs. Gray.

Jean. All that passed from that time to the time you quitted the house, Mr. Carnegie has heard.

Carn. Thank you; that's perfectly clear how he came to have on your clothes, and as he was about your size, and as his features were unrecognizable, that explains how his body was taken for yours. Now tell me, have you any suspicion as to who murdered him?

Jeam. I have my suspicion that the laird knows, if he would only tell!

Jean. I will go and force him to tell! Oh, Robin! Robin! Justice will yet be done you!   (*exit, L.*

Enter Girzie, excited, R.

Girzie. Oh, ye're here, Jeames Falcon! It's fine times ye hae gien us, and my poor Wattie to die for ye. Ohone! Ohone!   (*sitting down, wailing*

Jeam. Girzie, Wattie was the only companion and friend I had, when in sore trouble. Next to yourself, I think, he liked me best, and you cannot know how bitterly I feel your loss, thinking that I am in some way partly to blame for it.

Girzie. I'm no doitered, Jeamie, though I'm broken down sair with this, and I blame nobody but them who thought the foul thought, and struck the blow that robbed me o' my bairn.

Jeam. They shall pay for it, do not doubt that!

Girzie. Who? Carrach my brither or Nicol who's Wattie's faither!

Jeam. What! Carrach your brother, and the laird Wattie's father?

Girzie. Ay, there's the sting o't. On the one hand is my brither, on the other hand is his faither. Oh, the curse has followed him from his birth, and the sins of his parents on him, an' on them through him. *(rising with hands raised and teeth clenched)* But if I knew the truth I would hae justice!

Jeam. You shall know the truth before many hours pass.

Girzie. Give me hope o' that?

Jeam. You will, as sure as I am alive!

Girzie. *(taking packet out of her bosom)* Ay, the dead came to life the day. *(handing him it)* There, that's yours—they're letters o' your mithers.

Jeam. My mothers! *(looking at them*

Girzie. Aye, I nursed her when she was dying at Clashgirn. She gied me these, and told me to keep them, and no' to let anybody know I had them, but to gie them to ye if ever the day came ye should need t' e n.

Jeam. Why did you not give them to me before?

Girzie. I didna' come across them till noo. Weel, I'll awa'. Ohone, my Wattie! Ohone! *(exit, L.*

Jeam. *(aside)* What's this? My mother's dying statement, and the proof of my heirship to all the property of Clashgirn. O man, man, how you are steeped in devilishness! *(to Carnegie)* Did you know Hugh Sutherland?

Carn. Do you mean the former owner of Clashgirn?

Jeam. Yes, him.

Carn. To be sure I knew him, but that was about twenty years ago. What about him?

Jeam. Would you know his handwriting?

Carn. Aye, among that of a thousand.

Jeam. Are these letters written by him? *(showing them*

Carn. *(looking them over)* Aye, positively!

Jeam. That will do. *(exit, Carnegie, L.*

Enter Nicol, R.

Nicol. Od'! It's extraordinar'! I did not expect the pleasure of seeing you. A fine hobble you have brought us all into.

Jeam. Nicol McWhapple, I would speak with you.

Nicol. Od'! It's extraordinar'! What's wanting?

Jeam. Laird, people have told me before that you had wronged me.

Nicol. Folks say queer things in this world, Jeanie.

Jeam. But the queer things they hinted at, in this case, were true. Not very long ago I refused to listen to their suspicions, because I thought even listening to them was ingratitude to you. Now I know their suspicions to have been true. That packet which my dying mother entrusted to her nurse, was delivered to me. This is it in my hand. *(showing it*

Nicol. Oom-hoo! And who was it gave you those interesting papers? *approaching slily*

Jeam. Girzie Todd. *(Nicol tries to snatch them)* Back, or I'll brain you!

Nicol. I was just making fun when I pretended that I was going to snatch the papers from you. What do you tell me this story for? If you think it true, and can prove it, why do you not go to a lawyer at once, and set the beadles at my heels?

Jeam. Had you given me the Askaig Place when I asked for it you would have been safe to-day: as it is, your infernal trickery has so marred the dearest hopes of my life that I do not care a single straw for the wealth it is in my power to claim.

Nicol. (*ironically*) Very kind of you, that.

Jeam. I wish to make a bargain with you for Jeannie's sake. Clear Cairnieford of the false charge against him, for I believe you know the real culprit, and on the day he leaves the jail a free and unblemished man, I will deliver these papers to you to do with as you please. I will leave the country, and you will never hear of me or the Colin again.

Nicol. Had it not been for you I might have been safe and well to-day. But you have been like a stone around my neck from the first day I saw you. Every day and every hour you reminded me of what was past, and kept me in torture of fear for what might be to come, and now you upset all my schemes, and you now shake the terrors of the gallows in my face.

Jeam. I offer you the means to escape it.

Nicol. You cannot do that, and if you could I would not accept it from you. No, I'll stand my ground to the last, now; for I may as well die as lose everything I have spent my life to win.

Jeam. You have chosen your course, and you will find it a short one, for in an hour from this I'll have Carrach a companion.

Nicol. (*drawing dirk, and opening a small snuff box*) Hang me? You could not do that, you have not the power to do it. I am wrongfully accused. I'm a martyred man, but I'll have the law on you, sir—I'll have—— (*seeing Hutcheson, who advances*) Who is that?

Hutch. Take another pinch, laird, it will do you good.

Nicol. (*putting up box and dirk*) Who is that?

Jeam. A friend come to hear what information you have to give on this extraordinary smuggling business.

Nicol. I know nothing about it. (*trembling with fear*

Hutch. I should tell you, laird, that the only chance you have is to make a clean breast of it, and tell us everything.

Nicol. Do you really think that.

Hutch. I'm sure of it.

Nicol. And if I tell—that is if I had anything to tell—will it give me a chance to get out of the scrape?

Hutch. Surely, surely.

Nicol. They will not hang me, it was not me who did it. I'm an innocent man. Oh, what's that? They're coming! Oh, save me!

Girzie enters suddenly, Nicol kneels in terror before her.

Girzie. Ye're a puir miserable coward. How ye suffer; but ye hae brought it on yourself.

Nicol. (*rising disdainfully*) All what, woman? Are you mad? What's wrong?

Girzie. Everything's wrong. Fly, man, fly! They are on your heels!

Nicol. Who? Let them come on!

Girzie. Nae, I canna let them take ye, much wrongs as ye hae done me. Ye were the faither o' my dead Wattie, and must nae hang on the gallows if I can save ye. Come awa', there's maybe time yet.

Nicol. What are you raving at, woman? What do you mean?

Girzie. Mrs. Gray found the paper ye hid, signed by Carrach, and it tells how my poor Wattie was done to death, and oh, lord, it was by my ain brither's hand, and through your ill schemes.

Nicol. My God, woman!

Girzie. Ay, and they told me they were comin' to take ye prisoner, and that ye would be hanged. I was glad until I minded o' Wattie and I came to help ye rin awa' for his sake. Oh, Jeamie Falcon and your frien', if ever ye cared for my bairn, wha' died for ye, turn awa your faces that ye may nae be tempted to do your duty, and for his sake let me save his faither from a cruel death if ye can.

Jeam. We will, for Wattie's sake, Girzie. (*they turn their heads*

Girzie. Come awa' then, if ye want to live, we can get out o' this window afore they come. (*she seizes him by the waist*

Nicol. But, woman, I have not my money to take with me.

Girzie. Come awa', or the only money ye'll need will be as much as will buy a shroud.

She drags him too, and almost pushes him out of window, following herself.

Enter Smart, L.

Jeam. (*aside*) The fiscal! What am I to say to him?

Smart. Let them go. We have the true culprit safe, the laird will be punished enough by his own conscience. Now please stand to one side awhile.

Jeam. We will leave. (*exit with Hutcheson,* R.

Smart. (*opens back door and calls*) Cairnieford!

Enter Robin, C. D.

Robin. Is anything wrong, sir? Hae ye any news for me? Is my wife weel, or——

Smart. Quietly, Cairnieford. One question at a time, and before I say a word understand this, I am here as your friend, not as the fiscal.

Robin. I understand, sir, and thank ye, and ye may count on me laying nae stress on what ye may say if ye should need to alter your words hereafter.

Smart. That's right, and I'm glad that I have good news for you.

Robin. She's weel then? She'll come to see me again?

Smart. Your good wife? Oh, yes, she is finely, and I hope you'll be able to save her the trouble of coming to see you here, by going to see her.

Robin. Eh? What?

Smart. Now mind, it's Mathew Smart, not the fiscal speaking.

Robin. Ay, ay! I mind.

Smart. Well, then, there's been a mistake someway, the fiscal was misled by the information he got, so the chances are that as soon as the needful formalities are gone through with, you'll be set free.

Robin. Free?

Smart. Yes free, that's the word, and as clear of any suspicion of guilt as if you had never been here.

Robin. But how—how has it come about ?   I'm dazed by it a'—
it's sae sudden.

Smart. You have your wife to thank, and James Falcon.

Robin. Falcon?

Smart. Yes, just him.   It was not him, but Girzie Todd's lad,
Wattie, who was killed.   That was what misled me—I mean the
fiscal.

Robin. Heighho!   (*sighing*

Smart. Why, man, what's wrong with you?   I thought you
would have been leaping for joy, instead of that you look as though
I had brought you word that your execution would take place Friday.

Robin. Falcon's no' dead?

Smart. No—are you sorry for that?

Robin. Sorry?   The Lord forbid!   It's a shame for me to look
ungrateful; but, man, if you had borne what I hae on his account,
ye would nae find it an easy matter to accept sae much favor at his
hands.   Lord forgie me, but I amaist feel as though I would rather
hae been left here to die than owe my life to ought that he has done.

Smart. Hoots, man, that's not like you.   But you'll think better
of it before long, and I hope then you'll give the lad your hand and
say you are sorry for your mistake, as I have done with you.

Enter Monduff and Carnegie, R.

Robin. My wife, she hasna come wi' ye ?

Mon. No, you see she's had a great deal to do, and she has over-
worked herself.

Carn. You'll not be long until you see her, have no fear of that,
Cairnieford.   The woman who could do what she has for you, must
have that in her heart which will make her glad to welcome you
when she learns that you place value on her welcome.

Robin. Value on her welcome?   Oh, man, I care nought for a'
the world's welcome if she be nae one to say it's weel I hae been
spared—it's weel there's nae shame on me.

Mon. Yes, but remember how you parted from her, and then
set yourself with all your might to prove to her that whatever you
may have thought, felt or said, in passion, you see how false it all
was, now that you are calm.

Enter Jeamie, unobserved, R.

Robin. Thank ye, sir, for that; it gives me courage and hope
too.   I will prove to her that I know her worth, and how cruelly I
hae tried her.   But where is she?

Mon. Adam went back to his old home, and Mrs. Gray went
there with him.

Carn. And Jeamie Falcon turns out to be laird o' Clashgirn.

Mon. Son of Hugh Sunderland.

Robin. I suspected that, and I told ye o' t at the time they buried
the lady, but ye wouldna hear o' sic a thing.

Carn. What could I do on mere suspicion?   Besides, I must confess that I was deceived by the laird's saintly way—very much deceived.   (*seeing Jeamie*

Robin. Deceived?   Ah, so was I, to my shame.

Mon. I think it a duty you owe the poor lad and yourself, to
tell him so, for nothing will better satisfy the folk of your sorrows
for his misfortune.

Carn. And here he is ready. *(bringing Jeamie forward*

Robin. James Falcon, or Mr. Sunderland, as I understand ye
should be called now, will ye speak wi' me a minute? It's easier
to be forgiving in the depths o' shame than when we're in the
pride o' health and strength. I doubtna it's my fault, and partly
yours, that Wattie Todd's lying a corpse, and ye canna refuse to
hear me afore the sod is laid on him.

Jeam. I'm listening.

Robin. I want to ask a question first. Ye know what it is to care
mair for a body than for a' the world, and a' that's in't beside. Tell
me then if ye had been in my place at Brownie's Bite what would
ye hae done?

Jeam. I do not know.

Robin. If every thought ye had, had been linked to her; if every
hope had sprung frae her; if she had been light and joy and hame to
ye; if she had been a' that the heart could care for or head think about;
and ye had been cheated wi' suspicions o' her; poisoned wi' doubts
o' her by a lieing tongue and strange circumstances, tell me, sir,
what would ye hae done had ye been in my place?

Jeam. I would have been blind and mad as you were, I believe.

Robin. It was an honest man that answered me. Will ye tak'
my hand now, for I feel nae shame in asking ye to pardon whatever
wrong I hae done ye. *(offering his hand*

Jeam. *(taking it)* Hush, forget that if you can, let it be
buried in poor Wattie's grave, and some day, maybe years after
this, long weary years they may be to me, but happy ones to you, I
hope, perhaps you and your wife will be able to call me your friend.

Robin. I call ye that now, and I am grateful to ye for letting me
do it. I can feel something o' what ye hae sacrificed in helping me.
But, sir, when I thought ye were in trouble I sought to offer you
help, ye know how I was cheated, and I only ask ye to judge me
by what ye might hae thought and done under the same circumstances.

Jeam. I do that. I am glad you have called me friend, and I'll
try and prove myself worthy of the name by quitting the port as
soon as I can. She says it would be better so, and she is right. God
bless her!

Enter Adam and Jeannie, R.

Robin. Ye here, Adam?

Adam. *(stiffly)* I'm glad to see ye on the right side o' the jail,
sir.

Robin. Thank ye, Adam, though ye look as if ye're rather angry
at the sight o' me. Weel, ye had reason to be angry wi' me, but I
own I was in the wrong, and I hae suffered for it. Dinna bear ill
will against me longer than ye can help.

Adam. *(stiffly as before)* I bear nae ill will.

Robin. Where is Jeannie?

Adam. My dochter is here. *(pointing to her*

Robin. *(kneeling)* Jeannie, will naething move ye to forgive me?

Jean. *(raising him)* I have done that long since, Robin, for I
know you must have borne much sorrow, but—

Robin. Dinna say that. God knows what I have borne, and God
knows it was because ye were sae dear to me that I was sae blind.

Jeau. Your eyes, are they open now?

Robin. Ay!

Jean. You have no doubt left in your heart that I have told you the truth?

Robin. Ye mind me o' my ain shame, ye mind me o' my ain misery when ye ask that.

Jean. But it might rise between us again?

Robin. Ye winna trust me? Oh, woman, if there could be anything come atween us, the memory o' that wild night at Brownie's Bite would make me crush it aneath my foot, like the poison head o' a serpent!

Jean. I believe you, Robin; so there.   (*giving her hand*

Robin. And our frien', Jeamie?   (*turning to him*

Jean. Here is mine.   (*giving his hand*

Robin. And Adam?

Adam. Weel, here then.   (*giving his*

Maud. We'll all join hands, for we are all friends and brothers, since "we are all John Thomson's Bairns."

            (*all join hands and sing "Auld Lang Syne"*

TABLEAU—CURTAIN.

SYNOPSIS OF INCIDENTS.

ACT I.—*"It is an ill wind that blows naebody guid."* SCENE.—Portlap-pock pier. Yo-ho, yo-ho, my hearties! The fishwife's opinion as to sailing on Friday. The skipper Ivan's determination and oath. Robin expresses his admiration to Adam of his daughter. The laird and Jeanie come to an understanding. The lad and lass alone. "To make the crown a pound," Jeanie resolves to go to sea. Renewal of their troth-plight. Nicol arouses Carrach's hatred for the lad, and bespeaks him a berth. Girzie eavesdrops and smells mischief. "This last embrace my pledge shall be." The anchor's weighed. Friends bid good speed. The fishwife's warning. "The Colin is doomed." Departure of the vessel. Tableau.

Act II.—*There's as guid fish in the sea as has ever been caught."* SCENE.—Interior of the fisherman's cot. Jeamie's prophetic vision. The invalid and cripple bewail their ill-luck. The cow stolen away. The minister's consolation. "The Lord's will be done." Robin as a friend indeed. The laird and the skipper witness the misery they make. Girzie's warning fulfilled. The news broken to the lass. O woe is me! O woe is me! Jeannie inconsolable. Robin's proposal. A stern father's bidding obeyed. The auld farmer dances with joy. Jeannie crazed, sees her shipwrecked lover in her delirium. Tableau.

ACT III.—*"Better be off wi' the auld love afore ye are on wi' the new."* SCENE.—Brownie's Bite, and disclosed interior of Girzie's cot. Wattie, the human bellows, sees a ghost and gets a slap to bring him to his senses. The sailor lad's return. Ill news deferred. The blow struck, and Jeamie overcome. As false as fair. The dead come to life. Face to face. Love's despair and Fate's decree. The goodman's jealousy aroused by the hypocrite Nicol. The simpleton's persistance in following Jeamie. A clandestine meeting brought about by the laird and his lads. Robin discovers his wife and her lover under suspicious circumstances. The quarrel, the threat, and the curse. Out in the storm. "O woe is me!" The murder on the bridge. Tableau.

ACT IV.—*"It takes a wee spark to mak' a muckle bleeze."* SCENE.—Interior of the Port Inn. Gossips retailing the news. The fishwife inquiring the whereabouts of her son. Jeannie claims protection from her father. Meeting brought about by the minister. Explanation and recrimination. An unsuccessful attempt at reconciliation. Robin compels the laird to explain. Doubts encouraged and faith utterly lost. Nicol and Carrach have a settlement in full. The body found and the sheriff called. His verdict. The auld farmer and the lawyer consult. Business disturbed by Mathew and others. Robin Gray's arrest. Jeannie cast off. Tableau.

ACT V.—*"It's a lang lane that has nae end nor turning."* SCENE.—Sheriff's apartment in the jail. Jeannie examined and cross-questioned. An interview with her husband allowed, and interrupted. Carrach and his accomplices in the toils. The cat out of the bag. Jeannie recognizes the man who deceived her. "Murder will out." Jeannie's faith in her husband's innocence and her determination to prove it. Girzie deplores the loss of her simpleton child. The wrong man murdered. Jeannie appears to clear his rival and enemy of guilt. The crime brought home to its author, and the laird exposed. Just deserts given, and a happy reconciliation. "We're a' John Thompson's bairns."

————

Three months are supposed to elapse between the first and second acts, and one year between the second and third acts.

64. THAT BOY SAM. An Ethiopean Farce in one act, by F. L. Cutler. 3 male, 1 female character. Scene, a plain room and common furniture. Costumes, comic, to suit the characters. Very funny, and effectually gives the troubles of a "colored gal" in trying to have a beau, and the pranks of "that boy Sam." Time of performance twenty minutes.

65. AN UNWELCOME RETURN. A Comic Interlude. in one act, by Geo. A. Munson. 8 male, 1 female character. Scene, a dining room. Costumes. modern. Companies will find this a very amusing piece, two negroes being very funny—enough so to keep an audience in the best of humor. Time of performance, twenty minutes.

66. HANS, THE DUTCH J. P. A Dutch Farce in one act, by F. L. Cutler, 3 male, 1 female character. An exceedingly funny piece. Hans figures as a Justice in the absence of his master, and his exploits are extremely ludricous. Costumes modern. Scene, plain room. Time of performance,twenty minutes.

67. THE FALSE FRIEND. A Drama in two acts, by Geo. S. Vautrot. 6 male, 1 female character. Simple scenery and costumes. First class characters for leading man, old man, villain, a rollicking Irishman, etc. also a good leading lady. This drama is one of thrilling interest, and dramatic companies will invariably be pleased with it. Time of performance, one hour and forty-five minutes.

68. THE SHAM PROFESSOR. A Farce in one act, by F. L. Cutler. 4 male characters. This intensely funny afterpiece can be produced by any company. The characters are all first class, and the "colored individual" is especially funny. Scene, a plain room. Costumes, simple. Time of performance, about twenty minutes.

69. MOTHER'S FOOL. A Farce in one act, by W. Henri Wilkins. 6 male, 1 female character. Like all of Mr. Wilkins' plays, this is first class. The characters are all well drawn, it is very amusing, and proves an immense success wherever produced. Scene, a simple room. Costumes modern. Time of performance, thirty minutes.

70. WHICH WILL HE MARRY. A Farce in one act, by Thomas Egerton Wilks. 2 male, 8 female characters. Scene, a street. Costumes modern. Easily arranged on any stage. A barber hears that one of eight women has fallen heir to some money, not knowing which, he makes love to them all. This, together with the revenge the females have upon him, will prove laughable enough to suit any one. Time of representation, thirty minutes.

71. THE REWARD OF CRIME, OR THE LOVE OF GOLD. A Drama of Vermont, in two acts, by W. Henri Wilkins. 5 male, 3 female characters. A drama from the pen of this author is sufficient guarantee of its excellence. Characters for old man, 1st and 2d heavy men, juvenile. A splendid Yankee, lively enough to suit any one. Old woman, juvenile woman, and comedy. Costumes modern. Scene, plain rooms and street. Time of performance, one hour and thirty minutes. Easily placed upon the stage, and a great favorite with amatuers.

72. THE DEUCE IS IN HIM. A Farce in one act, by R. J. Raymond. 5 male, 1 female character. Scene, a plain room. Costumes modern. This farce is easily arranged, and can be produced on any stage, in fact, in a parlor. The pranks of the doctor's boy will keep an audience in roars of laughter, every line being full of fun. Time of performance, thirty minutes. Order this, and you will be pleased.

73. AT LAST. A Temperance Drama in three acts, by G. S. Vautrot. 7 male 1 female character. This is one of the most effective temperance plays ever published. Good characters for leading man, 1st and 2d villain, a detective, old man, a Yankee, and a capital negro, also leading lady. The temptations of city life are faithfully depicted, the effects of gambling, strong drink, etc. Every company that orders it will produce it. Costumes modern. Scene, Mobile, Time of performance, one hour and thirty minutes.

74. HOW TO TAME YOUR MOTHER-IN-LAW. A Farce in one act, by Henry J. Byron. 4 male, 2 female characters. Scene, parlor, supposed to be in the rear of a grocery shop. Costumes modern. Whiffles the proprietor of the grocery, has a mother-in-law who is always interfering with his busines. Various expedients are resorted to to cure her—a mutual friend is called in, who, by the aid of various disguises frightens the old lady nearly to death, finally Whiffles gets on a "ge-lorious drunk," and at last triumphs. A perfect success. Time of performance, thirty-five minutes.

75. *ADRIFT.* A Temperance Drama, in three acts, by Chas. W. Babcock, M. D. Six male, four female characters. Good characters for leading man, villain, comedy, juvenile, a capital negro, and jolly Irishman. Also leading lady, little girl, juvenile lady, and old negress. A deep plot, characters well drawn and language pure. Easily produced. Scenery simple and costumes modern. Time of performance, one hour and a half.

76. *HOW HE DID IT.* A comic Drama in one act, by John Parry, three male, two female characters. An amusing scene from real life. A plot is laid to cure a husband, who having lost a first wife whom he domineered over, tries to treat a second one in like manner. A splendid comedian's part. Time about thirty minutes. Costumes modern.

77. *JOES VISIT.* An Ethiopean burlesque on the Rough Diamond, two male, one female characters. Easily produced and very laughable. Can also be played white. Time twenty minutes. Costumes extravagant negro.

78. *AN AWFUL CRIMINAL.* A Farce in one act, by J. Palgrave Simpson, three male, three female characters. Plot excellent and its development very amusing. The oftener produced the better it is liked—is in one scene and easily put upon the stage. Costumes simple. Time thirty-five minutes.

79. *THE SPY OF ATLANTA.* A Grand Military Allegory in six acts, by A. D. Ames and C. G. Bartley, fourteen male, three females. This play is founded on incidents which occured during the war of the Rebellion—It introduces Ohio's brave and gallant McPherson—the manner of his capture and death. It abounds with beautiful tableaux, drills, marches, battle scenes, Andersonville, etc., and is pronounced by the press and public, the most successful military play ever produced. G. A. R. Posts, Military Companies and other organizations, who may wish something which will draw, should produce it. It may not be out of place to add that this play with the incidents of the death of McPherson, was written with the consent of the General's brother, R. B. McPherson, since dead, who fully approved of it. Price 25 cents per copy.

80. *ALARMINGLY SUSPICIOUS.* A Comedietta in one act, by J. Palgrave Simpson, four male, three females. This play is easily arranged, and the plot excellent. Some things are "Alarmingly Suspicious" however, and it will please an audience. Time forty-five minutes.

81. *OLD PHIL'S BIRTHDAY.* A serio-comic Drama in two acts, by J. P. Wooler, five male, two females. Scenery easily arranged. Costumes modern. One of the purest and most attractive plays ever published. The character of "Old Phil" cannot be excelled, and the balance are every one good. Time one hour and forty-five minutes.

82. *KILLING TIME.* A Farce in one act, one male, one female. Scene a drawing room. Costumes modern. A woman held captive at home by the rain seeks to "kill time." How she does it is told by this farce. Time about thirty minutes.

83. *OUT ON THE WORLD.* A Drama in three acts, five males, four females. Scenery not difficult. Modern costumes. A thrilling picture of love, fidelity and devotion. Excellent leading characters and Irish comedy, both male and female. Can be produced on any stage. Time two hours. An American Drama.

84. *CHEEK WILL WIN.* A Farce for three male characters, by W. E. Suter. Costumes modern. Scene plain apartment. It is said that nothing will carry a man through the world as well as plenty of "cheek." A striking example is given in this farce. It will please all. Time thirty minutes.

85. *THE OUTCAST'S WIFE.* A domestic Drama in three acts, by Colin H. Hazlewood, twelve males, three females. Costumes modern. A thrilling play of the blood and thunder order, abounding in exciting scenes, and hair-breadth escapes. Is a favorite wherever produced, and has leading man, old man, juvenile and comedy characters. The "wife" is a grand one for leading lady, and there is a good comedy. Time one hour and forty-five minutes.

86. *BLACK VS WHITE OR THE NIGGER AND YANKEE.* A Farce in one act, by Geo. S. Vautrot, four males, two females. Simple scenery. Modern costumes. In this farce is combined the Ethiopean and Yankee, both characters being very funny, as well as other excellent parts. Time of performance, thirty-five minutes.

87. *THE BITER BIT.* A Comedy in two acts, by Barham Livius, 5 male, 2 female characters. In-door scenes—costumes easily arranged. This is a most laughable comedy, and will please all who read it or see it performed. A fine lesson to married men who are a little wild can be learned from this comedy. Time of performance one hour and a quarter.

88. *THE MISCHIEVOUS NIGGER.* An Ethiopian farce in one act, by C. White, 4 male, 2 female characters, Antony Snow, the Mischievous Nigger, is a favorite with ethiopian comedians. Also good characters for old man, Frenchman, Irishman, Old Woman and Servant. Properties, scenery, costumes, etc. easily arranged. Time 25 minutes.

89. *THE BEAUTY OF LYONS.* A Domestic Drama in 3 acts, by W. T Moncrieff, 11 male and 2 female characters. It is impossible to give an idea of what this drama is in a small space. It is a beautiful play, with a deep plot, fine leading characters for male and female, with good old men, juveniles, etc. It sparkles with fine comedy, and the language is of a high order. It is not difficult to present. Costumes easily arranged. Time about 2 hours.

90. *NO CURE, NO PAY.* An Ethiopian farce in 1 act, by G. W. H. Griffin, 3 male, 1 female character. Costumes to suit the characters. Scene, a doctor's office. Very funny. Time of performance 15 minutes,

91. *MICHAEL ERLE, OR THE FAYRE LASS OF LICHFIFLD.* A Romantic drama in 2 acts, by Thomas Egerton Wilks, 8 male and 3 female characters. A thrilling melo-drama, which has been played with the greatest success by both professional and amateur companies in all parts of the U. S. and England. Costumes shape dresses, etc. Scenery, street, landscape and chamber. Good characters for all. Time of performance 1 ¾ hours.

92. *THE STAGE STRUCK DARKEY.* An Ethiopian interlude in 1 act. The name implies what the piece is. Very amusing. 2 male, 1 female character. Costumes "nigger." Scene, plain room. Time 15 minutes.

93. *THE GENTLEMAN IN BLACK, OR THE DESERTER.* A comic drama in 2 acts, by William H. Murray, 9 male, 4 female characters. This drama abounds with fine comedy, thrilling situations, storms, etc., etc., and does not fail to please an audience. The characters are good. A full description of costumes are given, which are not difficult to arrange. Time 1 ¼ hours.

94. *16,000 YEARS AGO.* A Negro farce in one scene, as originally produced by Buckley's Serenaders. Is very comical. Time of playing 10 to 20 minutes.

95. *IN THE WRONG CLOTHES.* An uproarously funny farce, in 1 act, by James Burton, 5 male, 3 female characters. This very laughable farce cannot be described in a few lines. The eight characters are all first-class, and the scrapes several of them get into will keep an audience convulsed with laughter. Costumes simple. Time 40 minutes.

96. *ROOMS TO LET WITHOUT BOARD.* An Ethiopian sketch in one scene, 2 male, 1 female. Very funny. Time 15 minutes.

97. *THE FATAL BLOW.* A Melo-Drama in two acts, by the ever popular author, Edward Fitzball, Esq, seven male and one female character. This author always writes good plays, and this is no exception. It is a great favorite with amateurs, as well as professionals, and is filled with startling situations of the "blood and thunder" kind. Costumes and scenery not very difficult. Time of performance, one hour and a quarter.

98. *THE BLACK STATUE.* An Ethiopian farce in one scene, by C. White, four male and two female characters. Very laughable and easily arranged. Time of representation about fifty minutes.

99. *JUMBO JUM.* An original farce in one act, as first produced at the Boston Theatre, four male and three female characters. Scenes simple and easily arranged. Costumes modern. Any one ambitious to play a first-class negro character, full of genuine fun and humor need look no further. It will keep an audience in roars of laughter. Time of performance about thirty minutes.